A flood of adrenaline surged through her.

Claire shoved through the glass doors and took off down the sidewalk toward the car. Mike must've seen her in the rearview mirror because the engine growled to life at her approach.

The man yelled after her, but she had no intention of stopping.

Despite her high-heeled boots, she took off in a run, someone sprinting behind her.

She tugged open the door and scrambled inside the car. The man had caught up with her and made a grab for her coat as it flew out behind her.

"Claire?" Mike's voice gave her strength and purpose.

"Go, Mike! Just go!"

That was all he needed from her. No questions, no answers.

He floored the gas pedal and the car lurched away from the curb, flinging the door open and shedding the government man hanging on to it.

SECRET AGENT SANTA

CAROL ERICSON

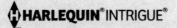

To Margery, hope this Christmas brings you fond memories

Recycling programs
for this product may
not exist in your area.

ISBN-13: 978-0-373-74924-9

Secret Agent Santa

Printed in U.S.A.

www.Harlequin.com

Carol Ericson lives with her husband and two sons in Southern California, home of state-of-the-art cosmetic surgery, wild freeway chases and a million amazing stories. These stories, along with hordes of virile men and feisty women, clamor for release from Carol's head. It makes for some interesting headaches until she sets them free to fulfill their destinies and her readers' fantasies. To learn more about Carol, please visit her website, carolericson.com, "Where romance flirts with danger."

Books by Carol Ericson

Harlequin Intrigue

Brothers in Arms: Retribution

Under Fire
The Pregnancy Plot
Navy SEAL Spy
Secret Agent Santa

Brody Law

The Bridge
The District
The Wharf
The Hill

Brothers in Arms: Fully Engaged

Run, Hide
Conceal, Protect
Trap, Secure
Catch, Release

Harlequin Intrigue Noir

Toxic

Visit the Author Profile page at
Harlequin.com for more titles.

CAST OF CHARACTERS

Claire Chadwick—A wealthy socialite obsessed with her husband's murder five years ago at the hands of terrorists. She stumbles upon a clue that links his death to a present-day terrorist plot and goes undercover with the one man who can save her life and help her slay the demons of her past.

Mike Becker—A covert ops agent, ready to retire after a mission gone bad, decides to go on one more assignment, which will prove to be his redemption...or his undoing at the hands of a beautiful socialite.

Senator Spencer Correll—Claire's stepfather might be guilty of more than being a greedy politician.

Shane Chadwick—A journalist and Claire's husband, who was murdered five years ago and might provide the key to Caliban's identity.

Hamid Khan—Claire sponsored this young man's immigration from Pakistan to the US, but his American Dream just might turn to ashes.

Lori Seaver—The nanny for Claire's young son is loyal and dedicated, but is she sleeping with the enemy?

Fiona Levesque—Senator Correll's secretary is a jilted lover and she wants revenge, even if that revenge puts her life in danger.

Caliban—The mysterious leader of Tempest—the black ops organization that's trying to throw world affairs into chaos—wants to rule the world and satisfy his vendetta against Jack Coburn and Prospero in the process.

Chapter One

Password Failed.

The message mocked her, and Claire almost punched the computer monitor. She didn't think it would be easy figuring out her stepfather's password, but she didn't think it would take her almost fifty tries over the course of three weeks, either. How did those hackers do it?

Placing her fingers on the keyboard, she closed her eyes, racking her brain for the next possible password. The voices in the hallway stopped her cold, sending a ripple of fear across her flesh.

She had no reason to be in this office, especially with a lavish party going on downstairs— *her* lavish party. She whipped her head around, the action loosening her carefully coiffed chignon, and lunged for the French doors. She parted the drapes, grabbed one handle and slipped through the opening onto the balcony.

She clicked the glass door shut just as she saw the door to the office crack open. Placing her palms against the rough brick, she sidled along the wall until she reached the edge of the balcony farthest from the doors.

Feathers of snow drifted from the night sky, leaving a dusting of white on the Georgetown streets. DC rarely saw snow in December. Just her luck.

She crossed her arms, digging her fingers into the cold skin exposed by her sleeveless gown. She couldn't stay here long or her stepfather's security detail would find her and would have to chip her stiff body from the brick facade of the town house.

The French doors next to her swung open and Claire flattened herself against the wall. Her stepfather, Senator Spencer Correll, must've noticed the parted drapes or the chill in the room and had decided to investigate. What possible excuse could she offer for being out on the balcony in the snow in an evening gown in the middle of a party?

"I love it when it snows in DC." Her stepfather's hearty tone reassured her that he had no idea anyone was lurking out here—it also sounded forced. He must be putting on an act for someone—but then, when didn't he put on an act?

"We're not going to have a white Christmas in South Carolina, so maybe I'll stay here for a week or two and soak up the atmosphere."

The other man's Southern drawl marked him as a constituent from her stepfather's home state. She just hoped the snow didn't enthrall him enough to step onto the balcony.

"I suggest you do. Nothing like Christmas in DC."

Spencer's voice sounded so close, she was surprised he couldn't see her breath in the cold air. She held it.

"It'll be an especially merry Christmas for you, Senator Correll, if you vote for that…uh…subsidy."

"It's a done deal. I'll introduce you to my assistant tonight. Trey will take care of all the details. After tonight, your boss should be reassured."

"Looking forward to it." The toe of a polished dress shoe tapped the pavers on the balcony, and Claire clenched her teeth to keep them from chattering.

"There's quite a crowd here tonight, Senator. I understand your stepdaughter, Claire, is an amazing fund-raiser."

"If by fund-raiser you mean relentless harridan, that's Claire." Spencer chuckled. "Just like her mother."

Claire's blood ran like ice through her veins, and it had nothing to do with her rapidly dropping body temperature. The chill in Spencer's voice when he mentioned her mother buoyed her suspicions that he'd had something to do with Mom's death. Maybe by discovering what he was up to with his vast amount of fund-raising and secretive meetings with suspected terrorists she would finally uncover evidence tying him to Mom's so-called accident.

She still had the video—the video that had sent her reeling and tumbling down a rabbit hole.

"A great lady, your wife." The shoe retreated, and Claire never heard Spencer's response to the compliment to his dead wife as the doors closed on the two men.

She let out a long breath and a new round of chills claimed her body. Even though they'd closed the door, her stepfather and his crony were still in the office.

She turned toward the low wall around the balcony and peered over the edge. She could hike up her dress and climb over and then try to reach the trellis that was positioned on the side of the building. She was just one story up.

"Are you going to jump?"

She gasped and jerked her head toward the sound of the voice from below. A man stood just outside the circle of light emanating from the side of the house. What was he doing out here? More important, why was he yelling? She put her finger to her lips and shook her head.

He caught on quickly. He shrugged a pair of broad shoulders draped in a black overcoat and turned the corner back to the front of the house, his red scarf billowing behind him.

Could this night get any worse? She rubbed

her freezing hands together, and couldn't feel her fingertips.

Then the shadows from the office stopped their dance across the balcony and she knew the two men had left the room. Biting her lip, she tried the door and heaved a sigh of relief. At least Spencer hadn't locked it. He didn't need to with the sensors, cameras and security guards monitoring this place—her place.

She tripped back into the room, her feet blocks of ice in her strappy silver sandals. She made a beeline for the door, throwing a backward glance at the computer. She'd finish checking passwords another time.

She crept down the hallway toward the stairs, but instead of heading down to her party, she climbed the steps to the third level of the expansive townhome her mother used to share with Spencer Correll, Mom's third husband.

She needed to warm up before mingling with her guests, anyway, and a visit to her son was a surefire way to warm both her heart and body.

Pushing open the door next to her bedroom, she tiptoed into the darkened room, the night-light shaped like a train her beacon. She knelt beside Ethan's bed and burrowed her hands beneath the covers, resting her head next to his on the pillow.

His warm mint-scented breath bathed her cheek, and she traced the curve of his earlobe with her lips.

She whispered, "Love you, beautiful boy."

His long lashes fluttered and he mumbled in his sleep. She had to get him out of here, out of this viper's nest. His grandparents had been clamoring to take him snowboarding in Colorado over the holidays, and even though this would be her first Christmas without him, she was making the sacrifice to protect him. He'd be leaving her in two days.

"Claire?" The shaft of light from the hallway widened across the floor.

Her stepfather's voice always made her skin crawl.

"I'm in here, Spencer."

"You have a surprise guest downstairs."

"I hope this guest came with his or her checkbook."

"Oh, I think he came with a lot more than that." Spencer stepped into the room. "Where have you been all night? I haven't seen you since the festivities kicked off with the tree lighting."

"I had a headache, and then I stopped in to see Ethan. I'm getting in some extra time with him before sending him off to his grandparents."

"I still can't believe you're parting with your son over Christmas."

"The Chadwicks haven't had him for the holidays—ever. They deserve that."

"They should've told that son of theirs to stay home once he had a baby on the way. If he couldn't keep out of harm's way for you, he owed that to his child."

"That's enough." She straightened up and pulled back her shoulders. "Shane was doing what he loved. His work was important to him. I don't want you ever to say anything like that in front of Ethan."

Spencer held up his hands. "I wouldn't do that. Now, come downstairs. They're getting ready to serve dinner, and you'll want to see this guest. Trust me."

She wouldn't trust her stepfather if he told her it was snowing outside after she'd just been standing in the stuff. She smoothed her hands across the skirt of her dress, flicking a tiny crystal of ice onto the floor, and joined him at the entrance to Ethan's room.

He closed the door and placed a hand on her bare back. "You're cold."

"I feel like I'm coming down with something." She shrugged off his clammy hand and headed for the curving staircase with Spencer close on her heels.

Did he suspect something?

With her fingertips trailing along the carved bannister, she descended into the warmth and chatter below. She scanned the room, her gaze skimming over glittering jewels and black bow ties. She didn't see any special guest—just a bunch of strangers with checkbooks.

Looking back at Spencer, she asked, "Where's this special guest?"

"You don't have to pretend anymore, Claire." He drummed his fingers along her shoulder. "He told us everything."

A knot twisted in her stomach. What kind of game was her stepfather playing this time?

From the step above her, Spencer leveled a finger toward the foyer. "There he is."

Claire's eyes darted among the faces of the strange men gathered in the foyer shedding coats, and then her breath hitched in her throat when she caught sight of a tall, dark-haired man unwinding a red scarf from his neck.

Had he seen enough of her on the balcony to identify her?

He must've felt her stare burning into him because at that moment, he glanced up, his eyes meeting hers and his mouth twisting into a half smile.

Spencer nudged her from behind. "Don't be shy now that the cat's out of the bag. Go greet your fiancé."

CLAIRE CHADWICK LOOKED like a ghost at the bottom of the staircase, her pale skin, blond hair and long, sparkling silver dress blending together to form a glittering cloud. Only her eyes, big, round and dark, stood out in relief.

Lola hadn't exaggerated her friend's beauty,

but Claire didn't have the look of a woman greeting her fiancé for the holidays. Of course, what did he expect of a novice? He'd have to take the reins here.

He dropped his scarf on top of his overcoat, resting in a maid's arms, and took the ticket from her fingers. Nudging his bag on the floor with the toe of his dress shoe, he asked, "Could you please check this, too?"

Straightening his cuffs, he descended the two steps from the foyer into the great room, decorated with twinkling lights and crystal stars hanging from the ceiling. An enormous Christmas tree dominated one corner of the room, coated with silver flocking and sporting gold ornaments amid its colored lights.

He made a beeline for Claire, taking tentative steps in his direction, her stepfather, Senator Spencer Correll, almost prodding her forward.

This scenario wasn't going as planned.

As the distance between them shortened to two feet, he held out one hand. "Sweetheart, I hope you don't mind that I surprised you like this. My conference ended early." He took her cold, stiff fingers in his hand and squeezed. "Lola sends her love."

He pulled Claire toward him and kissed her smooth cheek. At the mention of Lola's name, her hand relaxed in his. He didn't know where the communication had failed, but at least Claire had some expectation of his presence here.

Her arms twined around his neck and she pressed her soft lips against his. "Babe, I'm thrilled to see you here, even though you spoiled my surprise."

His arm curled around her slender waist, and they turned to face Spencer Correll together. Correll's assistant had joined them.

Mike stuck out his hand to introduce himself to the assistant, just to make sure Claire knew his name...or at least the name and identity he'd devised for this assignment. "Mitchell Brown, nice to meet you."

Correll clapped his hand on his assistant's shoulder. "Trey Jensen, this is Claire's fiancé, Mitchell Brown. Mitchell, my assistant, Trey Jensen."

He shook the other man's hand, already knowing his name, bank account balance and sexual predilections. "Good to meet you, Trey. Now, if you gentlemen don't mind, I'm going to steal my fiancée away from her own party for a few minutes."

Claire pinched his side. "I thought you'd never ask, babe."

Spencer chuckled. "You two go ahead. I'll hold down the fort for you, Claire. It's not like you've spent much time with your guests anyway."

Claire responded to this zinger by pulling Mike

toward the staircase with a firm grip. "We won't be too long."

They held hands up the stairs and across the landing until she dragged him into a library, its shelves lined with books and the floor covered by a thick carpet that muted their steps.

She shut and locked the door and then turned toward him, her unusual violet eyes alight with fire. "Fiancé? You're my fiancé?"

"I thought it was the best cover to keep me close to your side and privy to Correll's comings and goings. That way I can stay in this house. I even brought a bag. This is still your house, isn't it?"

"Yes." She narrowed her extraordinary eyes. "Did Lola send me someone I can actually work with, or a bodyguard?"

"Can't I be a little of both?" He spread out his hands. He liked it better when she had her arms curled around his neck, kissing him, instead of skewering him with a frosty gaze. He needed to get on her good side if he wanted her to give Lola a good report—not that it mattered at this point.

"Just so you know, Mitchell Brown is not my real name. It's Mike. Mike Becker."

"Suits you better." Crossing her arms, she tapped the toe of her glittering sandal. "When did this fiancé stuff all go down, Mike Becker?"

He put a hand in the pocket of his dress slacks and toyed with his coat-check ticket. "From the look on your face when I walked in, I figured you hadn't received Lola's final text."

"She told me she was sending someone from her husband's agency, but I didn't know the details. I certainly didn't know I was acquiring a fiancé."

"I didn't even give Lola all the details."

"I have a five-year-old son. To him, you'll be nothing but a friend, got it?"

The mama-bear attitude surprised him coming from this glittering goddess, but it figured she'd be protective of her son. He knew all about the boy and the tragic demise of her husband, Shane Chadwick.

"I know about…your son, and I have no intention of playing the doting fiancé or future stepdad in front of him."

She blinked and brushed a wisp of blond hair from her eyes. "Ethan's going out to his grandparents' place in a few days, anyway. I'm glad Lola gave you some background, although I'm sure you did some checking on your own."

"Of course." Didn't she realize that every covert-ops agent at home and abroad knew the story about her husband? Hell, didn't the entire world know? Mike cleared his throat. "Jack Coburn isn't too pleased you contacted his wife directly, but when you mentioned a connection between Correll and a terrorist group, we thought it best to investigate. You have some video proof?"

"I do. I'm sure it proves…something. You'll see." She'd hooked her finger around a diamond necklace encircling her neck, and the large pendant glinted in the low light of the library.

"When can I see it?" Jack wasn't all that convinced Claire had any proof of anything, but he didn't want to leave any stone unturned—especially when that stone involved his wife's friend.

"I have it in a secure location. I'll show it to you tomorrow."

"Your stepfather would be playing with fire if it's true. He has access to the highest levels of government."

"That's the scary part. My stepfather is a member of the Senate Intelligence Committee and was on the short list for director a few years ago. He still may be on that list."

"We'll get to the bottom of your suspicions one way or another."

Claire tapped her chin with two fingers, and a diamond bracelet matching the necklace slipped to her elbow. "I have more than suspicions. I'm almost positive Spencer is involved in terrorist activity."

"You'll have to give me more of the details, including that video, and I'll start digging around, but let's play the loving couple to establish my cover first—just not in front of your son." He straightened his bow tie as she wandered toward the window to gaze at the winter wonderland.

"You weren't going to jump from that balcony, were you?"

"So you did know that was me." She met his eyes in the glass of the window.

"Not when I first saw you outside, but I figured it out when I saw your dress. It's rather—" his gaze meandered from the hem of her full skirt to the top of the dress that had a deep V slashed almost to her waist "—distinctive."

"Well, I would hope so. I paid enough money for it." She tapped a manicured fingernail on the windowpane. "I was hiding from Spencer. I had been in his office trying out passwords to unlock his computer when he and some smarmy donor decided to have a meeting."

Whistling through his teeth, Mike joined her at the window. "Claire, why are you really after your stepfather? Most people don't see a few odd signs, a meeting on video with someone suspicious and immediately think 'terrorist plot.'"

"Just wait until you hear the whole story and see the videos before jumping to conclusions about me and my motives."

"Deal." He held out his hand and they shook on it. Still keeping her hand in his, he said, "Now, let's go downstairs and pretend to be a newly engaged couple."

Pointing out the window, she pressed her forehead against the glass. "Speaking of terrorism,

there's the director down there. Isn't he technically your boss?"

"Technically, although I've never met him and
most of what we do at Prospero is under the CIA
radar." He glanced into the street, where a bald-
ing man was exiting a town car as a valet held
open his door. "I'm surprised to see him at your
party. Didn't you have some beef with him a few
years ago?"

Another valet hurried to the front of the vehi-
cle, stooped over and then continued up the street
at a jog.

The hair on the back of Mike's neck quivered
at about the same time one of the director's security detail lunged across the car toward his charge.

Mike instinctively grabbed Claire around the
waist and yanked her away from the window just
as the explosion shattered the glass and rocked
the town house.

Chapter Two

Claire landed on the floor with Mike's body on top of hers. Acrid smoke billowed into the room from the shattered window and her nostrils twitched.

Mike's face loomed above hers, his mouth forming words she couldn't hear over the ringing in her ears. Sprinkles of glass quivered in his salt-and-pepper hair like ice crystals, and she reached out to catch them on the tips of her fingers.

The crystals bit into her flesh and she frowned at the spot of blood beading on her fingertip.

Mike rose to his knees over her and dragged her across the carpet, away from the jagged window. She couldn't breathe. Cold fear began to seep into her blood.

Rolling to her stomach, she began to crawl toward the door.

Mike's voice pierced her panic. "Claire. Are you all right?"

Cranking her head over her shoulder, she had enough breath left in her lungs to squeeze out one word. "Ethan."

Mike jumped to his feet and hooked her beneath her arms, pulling her up next to him. "Where is he?"

She pointed to the ceiling with a trembling finger, and then launched herself at the door of the library, her knees wobbling like pudding.

Mike followed her upstairs, keeping a steadying hand on the small of her back. Through her fog, Claire heard shrieks and commotion from downstairs. The noise shot adrenaline through her system, and she ran up the rest of the stairs to Ethan's room.

She shoved open the door and rushed to her son's bed, where he sat up rubbing tears from his eyes.

"Mommy?"

She dived onto the bed and enveloped him in a hug, blocking the cold air breezing through one shattered window. "Are you hurt?"

Shaking his head, he wiped his nose across her bare arm. "That was loud."

"That *was* loud." She kissed the top of his head, her gaze taking in Mike hovering at the door of the bedroom. "Don't worry. It was just an accident outside. Are you sure you're okay?"

Ethan disentangled himself from her arms and fell back against his pillow. "Uh-huh. Can I look out the window to see the accident?"

"Absolutely not. There's glass all over the floor. I'm going to move you to another bedroom across the hall, as long as there are no broken windows on that side."

Ethan squinted and pointed at Mike. "Who are you?"

"Pointing is rude." She grabbed his finger and kissed it. "That's my friend Mr. Brown."

Ethan waved. "Hi, Mr. Brown. Did you see the accident?"

Mike took two steps into the room accompanied by the sound of sirens wailing outside. "No, but I heard it. You're right. It was loud."

Ethan's nanny stumbled into the room, her hands covering her mouth. "Ethan? Oh, Claire, you're here. What was that?"

Claire held a finger to her lips. "Just an accident outside, Lori. Did the windows shatter in your room on the other side?"

"No. Do you want me to take Ethan to the room next to mine?"

"I'll come with you, and then I'd better see what's going on downstairs." Claire pulled Ethan from his bed and stood up with his legs wrapped around her waist. "Lori, this is Mitchell Brown, a friend of mine."

Lori's eyes widened. "Oh, I heard…"

Claire gave a jerk of her head, sending her chignon tumbling from its pins, and Lori sealed her lips.

"Yes, I heard you were here, Mr. Brown." Lori spun around and led them down the hall and around the corner to the other side of the town house.

She opened the door to the room next to her own.

Mike stayed outside in the hallway while Claire tucked Ethan into the queen-size bed and patted the covers. "Don't go back to sleep, Lori. I have no idea how extensive the damage is. The fire department may not even let us stay here tonight."

Lori gripped her arms and shivered. "As if I could go to sleep." She glanced at Ethan snuggling against the pillows and whispered, "Was that a bomb?"

Claire nodded.

Lori slumped in a chair across from the bed. "I'll stay here until you get back."

"I appreciate it, Lori." Claire closed the door with a snap and leaned against it, closing her eyes.

A rough fingertip touched her cheek, and her eyes flew open.

Mike raised his dark eyebrows over a pair of chocolate-brown eyes. "Are you ready?"

"He's dead, isn't he?" She grabbed the lapel of his dinner jacket. "The director is dead, along with his security detail and probably that valet."

"Most likely." He took her hand. "Let's go see if anyone else is."

He kept hold of her hand down the two flights of stairs and into the chaos that reigned in the great room. Even though she'd just met him, the pressure of his fingers kept her panic in check.

They reached the great room, and the glass that littered the floor crunched beneath their shoes. All the windows had been blown out, and snow swirled into the room.

Claire staggered, but Mike caught her and tucked her against his side. She cranked her head back and forth, but she could barely make sense of the scene before her.

Mike grabbed the arm of a passing fireman. "Are there any serious injuries?"

"Nothing too bad, no fatalities." He grimaced. "At least not on the inside."

She didn't even have to ask him if the director of the CIA had survived the blast—nobody in his position could have survived.

"Claire!" Spencer, his shirtfront bloodied, shouldered his way through the crowd. "Claire, are you and Ethan okay?"

All she could think about when she looked into his cold, blue eyes was that he was at the top of the list to replace the director. "We're fine. How about you?"

"Me? I'm indestructible."

"What happened?"

Mike squeezed her waist. They hadn't even discussed whether or not they'd reveal what they'd seen out the window, but instinct screamed *no* and Mike seemed to approve of her discretion.

She didn't want to be questioned as a potential witness, and Mike's real identity would have to be revealed if he stepped forward.

Dipping his head, Spencer pinched the bridge of his nose. "Oh, my God, Claire. It was a car bomb. Jerry..."

"Jerry Haywood? It was his car? Is he all right?" She dug her fingers into her stepfather's arm—as hard as she could.

He laid his hand on hers. "I'm afraid not, Claire. Jerry's dead, one of his security guys is dead and a valet."

"One of his security guys? Doesn't he usually travel with two? And is the other one okay?"

"He'd already stepped away from the car. He's injured but hanging on." He patted her hand again and then pulled away from her death grip.

"What about the other valet?" Mike stepped aside to let an EMT get by. "I noticed two tonight when I arrived."

"You know, I'm not sure about him. I'm going to make some inquiries. And stay tuned. The fire marshal may kick us all out of here tonight even though it's just broken windows." Spencer chucked Claire beneath the chin and made a half turn. His gaze lit on Mike's hair, still sprinkled with glass. "Where were you two?"

"In the library." Claire kicked a shard of glass to the edge of the floor.

"That's at the front of the town house. Were

you standing at the window by any chance? Did you see the explosion?"

Mike slipped his arm around her shoulder and kissed the side of her head. "We were too wrapped up in each to see anything."

Spencer's eyes narrowed briefly before he launched back into the crowd of people, shouting orders.

Claire blew out a breath. "There goes the new director of the CIA."

MIKE CUPPED THE cell phone against his ear. "If Senator Spencer Correll becomes the next director and he is involved somehow with a terrorist organization, we're going to have a major problem on our hands."

"That's an understatement," Jack Coburn's voice growled over the line. "How valid are Claire's concerns? Has she shown you her so-called evidence yet? I sent you out there to appease my wife and calm the fears of one of her best friends. I didn't believe she had anything— until this car bombing tonight."

Mike winced. Why *would* Jack send him on one last important mission after how badly he'd flubbed his previous assignment? Looking after Jack's wife's friend was just about his speed now.

He coughed. "I agree. After tonight's bombing, I'd say Claire might be onto something."

"Unless…" Jack sucked in a breath.

Mike's grip tightened on the phone. "Are you implying Claire set something up to bolster her story? That's crazy."

"After the murder of Claire's husband, she had it in for Jerry Haywood when he was deputy director."

"I know that, but it's a huge leap to think she'd plan his assassination."

Jack grunted. "Why would Correll be involved in an assassination at his own party?"

"Technically, it was Claire's party, and that's what I'm here to figure out, right? That's why you sent me." Mike sat on the edge of the bed in the room next to the one where Claire and her son were sleeping.

Since the bomb hadn't done any outward damage to the town house except for the broken windows, the fire department had allowed the family to stay the night. Workers had been busy boarding up the windows, and the DC Metro Police, the FBI, the CIA and a swarm of reporters were still milling around at the site of the car bomb.

Jack cleared his throat. "Just a warning about Claire Chadwick. She's had it pretty rough the past five years with the gruesome death of her husband and then her mother's accident. She blames her stepfather for her mother's death. You know that, right?"

"Lola mentioned something about it. Do

you think that makes Claire's suspicions about Correll's current activity invalid?"

"Not invalid, but she does have another agenda, a definite ax to grind. Her troubles have led to some...instability. Just be careful, and don't get sucked in by her beauty. From what I remember, Claire Chadwick's a real looker."

He'd remembered right. "Duly noted, boss."

"You sure you still want to retire, old-timer?"

A soft knock at Mike's door saved him from reciting all his reasons for retirement again to Jack. "Someone's here. Gotta go."

He pushed off the bed and padded on bare feet to the door. He cracked it open.

Claire, her disheveled hair tumbling over one shoulder, crossed her arms over her animal-print pajamas and hunched her shoulders. "Can I come in?"

"Of course." He swung the door open and stepped to the side.

"You weren't sleeping." Her gaze swept over his slacks and unbuttoned white shirt.

"I was on the phone." He closed the door behind her. "How's your son?"

"He's fine—sleeping. All he knows is that there was an accident that broke a bunch of windows in the house." She sat on the foot of the bed and then fell back, staring at the ceiling, her blond hair fanning out around her head. "Spencer did it. He's responsible."

As much as he wanted to join her on the bed, he parked himself on the arm of a chair across from her, resting his ankle on one knee. "You have one video of him meeting with a suspicious person and all of a sudden he's guilty of killing the CIA director?"

"It's more. It's a feeling." She hoisted herself up on her elbows.

"Whether Correll is responsible or not, this attack is bold, hits right at the heart of our security. If they can kill the director of the CIA in the middle of Georgetown, what else do they have planned?"

Her eyebrows shot up. "Something more? Do you think other attacks are planned?"

"There has to be some endgame here, and if your stepfather is involved somehow and can lead us to—"

"Shh." She put a finger to her puckered lips.

He cocked his head, holding his breath, and heard the wood creak on the other side of the door.

Claire bolted from the bed, launching herself at the door, but Mike caught her around the waist before she reached it. He swung her into his arms and sealed his lips over hers.

He groaned, a low guttural sound that was only half pretense as he felt her soft breasts beneath her silk pajama top press against the thin cotton of the T-shirt covering his chest.

He moaned her name against her luscious lips. "Claire. Claire."

She sighed and answered him in a breathy tone. "Mmm. Mitchell."

The board outside the room squeaked again, but he tightened his hold on Claire as she made a move toward the door.

Would he have to kiss her again to keep her from bursting into that hallway? It was better to err on the side of caution, so he backed her up against the door and took possession of her lips once more.

She placed her hands against his chest as if to push him away, but her fingers curled against the material of his T-shirt instead.

He kissed her long enough for whoever was outside that door to walk away—and then some. He raised his head, and she blinked her violet eyes.

Reaching around her, he opened the door. In a loud voice, he said, "Go back to Ethan. I'll be right next door all night."

"I'm so glad you're here, Mitchell." She peered down the hallway and shook her head. "I'm just sorry it couldn't have been a happier reunion."

He clicked the door behind her and fell across the bed, inhaling the sweet musky scent she'd left behind.

His first meeting with Claire Chadwick couldn't have been any happier.

Chapter Three

Claire fluffed Ethan's hair as she sat on the edge of the bed where she'd spent a sleepless night next to her squirmy son. If Mike had let her fling open the door, she might've caught Spencer in the act of eavesdropping.

And then what? He'd be alerted to her suspicions. Right now he suspected her only of nosing around his finances, and she wanted to keep it that way. Mike had been right to stop her.

But did he have to stop her by kissing her silly? She traced her mouth with her fingertips. Not that she'd minded.

Her son fluttered his long lashes and yawned.

Typically, Ethan woke up with the early birds, but last night's commotion had him sleeping late. Commotion? Was that what you called the murder of a CIA director by the man who would replace him? She had no doubt that was what had gone down. Now she just had to convince Mike Becker.

She hadn't trusted Spencer Correll since the fourth or fifth year of his marriage to her mother.

She'd been in college at Stanford when her mother married Spencer. Claire hadn't given him much thought. He was the type of man her mother had dated since Dad's death—charming, a few years younger, in need of some financing.

Despite her wariness, nothing set off any alarm bells until that phone call and then her mother's accident.

"Mommy?"

"Good morning, sleepyhead." She skimmed her fingers through Ethan's curly brown hair. "It's late."

His eyes grew round. "Can I look at the accident now?"

"I think that's been all cleaned up." At least she hoped to God it had been. "Let's have some breakfast. Are you hungry?"

"Uh-huh." He smacked his lips. "Is Mr. Brown eating breakfast, too?"

"You remember Mr. Brown from last night?" She tilted her head, wrinkling her nose. Mike must've made quite an impression on Ethan, which meant she couldn't get her son out of here and with his grandparents fast enough. She didn't want to confuse him or get his hopes up.

"Mr. Brown was giant, like Hercules." Ethan raised his hand over his head as far as he could.

"Yeah, he's tall." She grabbed him under the arms and tickled. "Now let's go eat."

The smells of bacon and coffee coming from

the kitchen lent an air of normalcy to the house after Claire had made her way through the cleaning crews in the great room. The giant Christmas tree she'd lit up with a thousand bulbs last night had shed its gold ornaments in the blast and now stood in the corner, a forlorn reminder of the Christmas spirit.

Ethan had shoved through the dining room doors first and came to a halt in front of Mike, his plate piled high with eggs, bacon and Jerome's flaky biscuits.

Mike eyed Ethan over the rim of his coffee cup. "Who are you, the cook?"

Crossing his arms, Ethan stamped his foot. "I'm Ethan. I saw you last night."

"Oh." Mike snapped his fingers. "You looked a lot smaller in bed. I thought you were a little boy, but you're not. You're a big boy."

Claire pulled out a chair with a smile on her face. Mike must have kids of his own, and if he wasn't divorced, he should be after the way he'd kissed her last night. No happily married man would be kissing a woman he'd just met like that—assignment or no assignment.

Ethan climbed into the chair next to Mike's, studied his plate and proceeded to ask Liz, the maid, for the same food Mike had.

Claire tilted her head at her son. "Are you sure you can eat that much?"

"I'm hungry." Ethan patted his tummy.

"How's your nose? Any sniffles or coughing?"

"Nope."

She turned to Mike. "Ethan's been having some problems with allergies, and the doctor is thinking it might be asthma."

"He looks good to me." Mike winked at Ethan.

"Ms. Chadwick, do you want anything besides coffee this morning?" Liz poured a stream of brown liquid into her cup.

"Just some orange juice." When Liz finished pouring the coffee, Claire tipped some cream into her cup and dipped a spoon into the white swirl.

"Did you get a good night's sleep despite everything?" Mike broke open a biscuit, and steam rose from the center.

Did he mean despite the murder of the director, or the kiss? She watched his strong hands as he buttered one half of the biscuit, then tore off a piece and popped it into his mouth.

Swallowing hard, she shook her head. "I didn't get much sleep at all. You?"

"Slept like a baby." He winked at Ethan again, who giggled.

"You're not a baby." Her son jabbed a fork in Mike's direction.

Claire drew her brows together as she glanced at Ethan's eyes, shining with clear hero worship. Since he'd started kindergarten a few months ago, Ethan had been asking more questions about his father and had become more aware of the absence of a father in his own life. She didn't want him getting too attached to Mike, especially since he'd seemed to form an immediate liking for him.

Like mother, like son.

"I don't even know why anyone would say they slept like a baby when they slept well." She pinched Ethan's nose. "Because you certainly didn't sleep all through the night when you were a baby."

Ethan giggled again and Mike added his loud guffaw just as Spencer walked into the dining room.

He raised his brows. "What a nice family scene, especially on a morning like this."

Claire jerked her head around, her finger to her lips. "Shh. Not now."

Spencer shrugged and refilled the coffee cup in his hand. He took a seat across from her. "When do you plan on telling him?"

"In our own time, Spencer." She sent Mike a look from beneath her lashes. "Did you learn anything more about what happened last night?"

"The Security Council had an emergency meeting this morning, and the FBI gave us an initial report."

She folded her hands around her cup, trying hard not to break it. "Anything you can pass along? Has anyone claimed credit?"

"Not yet." Spencer slurped at his coffee. "Too bad this had to spoil your visit, Mitch."

Mike reached across the table and curled his fingers around Claire's. "I don't plan on letting it ruin my visit. Of course, it's a tragedy, and I'm sorry it happened in front of your house, at Claire's event, but nothing can get in the way of our happiness."

She sent Mike a weak smile. He was really laying it on thick.

"My house?" Spencer folded his arms on the table. "Is Claire hiding assets from you already?"

"Sir?" Mike's fingers dug into her hand.

"This house belongs to Claire." Spencer spread his arms. "This house and everything in it."

"Mitchell and I haven't gotten around to detailing our assets yet." Heat crept up her chest and she took a gulp of chilled orange juice to keep it in check. She and Mike should've been covering this ground last night. Nothing much got past Spencer.

"Our—" Mike slid a glance at Ethan, busy marching his dinosaurs over a mound of scrambled eggs on his plate "—courtship was fast."

"I have to admit, when you showed up last night, it was the first I'd heard of you, but then, Claire plays it close to the vest. So your announcement didn't surprise me in the least, and it was quite welcome."

"I'm glad you approve." Mike gave her fingers one last squeeze before releasing her hand. "Are we still on for sightseeing today, or did the…accident change our plans?"

"I don't see any reason why your plans should change." Spencer pushed back from the table. "You might find a few monuments closed for security reasons, and you might have to drive through a few security checkpoints."

"Maybe we'll take a drive down to Virginia, Mount Vernon." She tugged on Ethan's ear. "You're going to Mallory's birthday party today."

Ethan dropped his dinosaurs. "She's gonna have cupcakes. She told me at school."

"And pony rides." She handed Ethan a napkin. "Wipe your face and I'll help you get ready to go."

Mike placed his own napkin by the side of his plate and smiled at Ethan. "Will you bring me a cupcake?"

"Yes. What color?"

"Surprise me."

Spencer hunched forward and whispered, "I think we should send some security with Ethan and Lori to that party. Just to be on the safe side."

She nodded. One more reason to get Ethan out of this town—and away from Spencer; not that her stepfather would ever hurt her son, but his connections might not be so sensitive.

FORTY-FIVE MINUTES LATER, Claire was staring out the car window at a gray sky threatening another dusting of snow. She shivered and wound her blue scarf around her neck.

"Are you cold?" Mike's fingers hovered at the dial of the car heater. "I can turn it up."

"I'm fine." She crossed her arms. "I'm just thinking about my stepfather sitting at that security meeting this morning, blood on his hands."

"How can you be so sure he's responsible, Claire? A few overheard conversations and a few suspicious emails don't prove anything concrete, and we need concrete."

"Be patient. You're here, aren't you? What I told Lola must've been convincing enough for her husband to send you out here to investigate."

His gaze narrowed. "Do you want the truth?"

"Considering you're my fiancé, that would be nice." She batted her eyelashes at him.

"Funny." He turned down the heat. "The truth is, you're Lola's friend. She's worried about you."

She clenched her teeth to keep her jaw from dropping. After a few deep breaths, she smoothed her hands over the pressed denim covering her thighs and then clasped her knees. "Are you telling me that none of you believe my stepfather is up to his neck in something nefarious? The CIA director was just murdered—in front of my house on his way to our party."

"Which may or may not have anything to do with Spencer Correll."

A sharp pain stabbed her between the eyes, and she pinched the bridge of her nose. "Are you here to help find evidence against my stepfather, or to play fiancé and protector to the poor, addled widow?"

"A little of both." He held up his hand when she took a breath, clenching her fists in front of her. "Nobody thinks you're poor and addled—especially not poor."

"You're insulting." She blew out a breath and flicked her fingers in the air. "Turn around. The engagement is over, and you can leave."

He raised his eyebrows. "That was insulting? I admit I'm brusque, comes from living in a world of subterfuge and secrets. When I have the opportunity to tell the truth, I take it. You want the truth, don't you?"

"Lola doesn't believe me?" Her nose stung. Lola Coburn was one of her oldest and best friends. She knew Lola had been concerned about her after Shane's…death, but Lola had sounded so sincere on the phone.

"Lola believes you have every right to suspect Spencer of complicity in your mother's death."

"But not that he's involved with a bunch of terrorists?"

"Nobody is dismissing that out of hand, Claire, and yes, the director's murder is convenient for Senator Correll."

"But…"

"No buts. I'm here to look into everything."

"Including my mental health." She scooted forward in her seat and tilted her head at him. "Why did Jack Coburn send one of his agents on what could very well be a wild-goose chase?"

"The truth again?"

"Why not? We seem to be on a roll."

"I'm retiring. I've been in this business too long, and I'm on my way out."

She scanned the touch of gray in the black hair at his temples and the lines in his rugged face. "So Jack asked if you'd mind checking in on the poor, addled widow on your way out?"

He reached out as quickly as a cat and chucked her beneath the chin. "Would you stop calling yourself that? You're not poor or addled."

"I know, I know, especially poor."

Tapping the car's GPS, he said, "Are we still going to Mount Vernon?"

"Why not? I just want to get out of DC, and Mount Vernon's as good as anyplace. Besides, I'm supposed to be showing you the sights."

"It's going to be a madhouse in DC for the next several weeks. Director Haywood's death is going to affect us, too."

"I think his assassination serves many purposes. I have no doubt that it was to put Spencer in position, but there must've been another reason. Maybe the director knew something." She squeezed her eyes closed trying to remember the last time her stepfather and Haywood had met.

"This is a lot bigger than you now, Claire.

You're not going to discover anything the CIA or FBI isn't going to discover."

"Is that your way of telling me to back off?" She gripped her knees, her fingers curling into the denim of her jeans. "If the CIA and the FBI had anything on Spencer, they would've made a move by now. I know things those agencies don't know."

He glanced at her as he veered off the highway, following the sign pointing toward Mount Vernon. "That's why I'm here."

They rode in silence as he maneuvered the car to the parking area. He swung into a slot, leaving a few spaces between her car and the next one over. "Not very crowded today."

"Too cold, and maybe people don't want to be hanging around tourist areas after last night."

"Do you want to head inside the mansion or get a cup of coffee at the Mount Vernon Inn so we can talk?"

"Since I dragged you out here so we could talk away from prying eyes and pricked ears, let's get some coffee."

Claire opened her door and stepped onto the parking lot, the heels of her knee-high boots clicking dully against the asphalt. The bare trees bordering the lot gave them a clear view of the mansion and the shops and restaurant next to it. "I don't think I've ever seen it so empty here."

"That's a good thing. The last time I visited, I couldn't get a table at the restaurant."

"I don't think we're going to have that problem now." She shoved her gloved hands into the pockets of her coat and hunched her shoulders. "Shall we?"

Mike locked the car and joined her, his own hands concealed in his pockets. They passed just two other parties making their way to the mansion.

Mike opened the door of the restaurant and ushered her into the half-empty room with its Colonial decor. A hostess in Colonial dress, a little white mob cap perched on her curls, smiled. "Do you have reservations?"

Raising his brows, Mike's gaze scanned the room. "No. Do we need one? We just want some coffee."

"Just checking. You don't need a reservation today." She swept her arm across the room. "We've had several cancellations. I think it's because of that awful business last night."

"You might be right." Mike nodded. "Can we grab that table by the window?"

"Of course."

They sat down and ordered their coffees, which their waitress delivered in record time.

Mike dumped a packet of sugar into the steaming liquid and stirred. Then he braced his forearms on the table, cupping his hands around the mug of coffee. "Start from the beginning."

"The beginning." Claire swirled a ribbon of

cream in her coffee and placed the spoon on the saucer with a click. "It all started when Spencer Correll came out of nowhere, married my mother and then killed her."

"Your mother fell down the stairs."

She took a sip of her coffee and stared at Mike over the rim of her cup. "He murdered her."

"You think he pushed her down the stairs? That's hardly a surefire method for murder. People can and do survive falls like that."

"He pushed her and then finished the job by smothering her with a pillow." Her eyes watered, and she dabbed the corners with her napkin.

"And you know this how?"

"I saw the pillow." She dashed a tear from her cheek.

"Lying next to your mother's body? What did the police think about it?"

"No, no." She took a deep breath. "That's just it. There was no pillow there. I noticed my mother's pillow on her bed later—with her lipstick on it."

"What is that supposed to mean?" Mike cocked his head, his nostrils flaring.

"My mother was meticulous about her beauty regimen." As Mike shifted in his seat, she held up her index finger. "Just wait. She never, and I mean never, went to bed with makeup on. She'd remove it, cleanse, moisturize. I mean, this routine took her about thirty minutes every night. There is no way there would be lipstick on her pillow, no reason for it."

"Let me get this straight." Sitting back in his chair, Mike folded his arms over his chest. "Your mother loses her life falling down some stairs, you see lipstick on her pillow and immediately believe your stepfather murdered her?"

"It wasn't just the pillow." She glanced both ways and the cupped her mouth with her hand. "It was the phone call."

"You just lost me." He drew his brows over his nose. "What phone call?"

"A few years before Mom's so-called accident, a woman called me with a warning about Spencer Correll. She said he was dangerous and that he'd killed before and would do so again to get what he wanted."

"Who was the woman?"

"She wouldn't give me her name."

"Did you inform the police?"

"At the time of the call?" She widened her eyes. "I thought it was a prank, but I told them about it when Mom died."

"They dismissed it."

"Yes, even after I showed them the pillow."

He rubbed his knuckles across the black stubble on his chin. "Did the cops tell Correll about your suspicions?"

"No."

"Did you ever hear from this woman again? After your mother's death?"

"No."

He dropped his spikey, dark lashes over his eyes, but not before she saw a glimpse of pity gleaming from their depths.

She clenched her jaw. She didn't expect him to believe her, but she didn't want to be pitied. People generally reserved their pity for the crazy or delusional. Neither applied to her—anymore.

He huffed out a breath and took a sip of coffee. "So, you believe your stepfather killed your mother, but how in the world does that link him to terrorists?"

Pursing her lips, she studied his lean face, his dark eyes bright with interest. At least he hadn't called for the little men in the white coats yet. "I didn't say the murder had anything to do with terrorism, but it prompted me to start nosing around his personal effects."

"What did you discover?" He gripped the edge of the table as if bracing for the next onslaught of crazy.

She reached into her bag and pulled out the envelope containing the picture, the picture she'd taken from the video she rescued from the trash can on Spencer's computer. She pinched it between two fingers and removed it from the envelope. Then she dropped it on the table and positioned it toward Mike with her fingertip.

Picking it up, he squinted at the photo. "It's your stepfather talking to another man. Who is he?"

"He's the terrorist who killed my husband."

Chapter Four

Mike's gaze jumped to Claire's flushed face, her violet eyes glittering with a challenge, her lips parted.

She'd really gone off the deep end. Nothing she had to say about Correll could be of any importance now. A hollowness formed in the pit of his stomach, threatening to engulf him.

How could he possibly save this bright, beautiful, damaged woman?

He toyed with the corner of the picture, a piece of paper really, with the image printed on it. "How do you know this man is the one who killed your husband? On the video, your husband's executioner was masked."

"Do you know how many times I watched that video? It's seared into my brain."

Swallowing, he grabbed her hand. "Why? Why torture yourself?"

"My torture paled in comparison to the torture Shane endured." She blinked her eyes, but no tears formed or spilled onto her flawless skin. "I watched that video frame by frame. I memorized every detail about that man, mask or no mask."

"You really believe this man—" he flicked the edge of the paper "—is the same man in the video with your husband."

"I'm sure of it."

Her voice never wavered, her eyes never lost their clarity.

"Why?" He loosened his grip on her hand and smoothed the pad of his thumb over her knuckles. "Explain it to me."

"This—" she tapped her finger on the picture "—is a still from a video I found on Spencer's laptop. It's the video I was telling you about before. I have the entire thing. I can see the way the man moves, the tilt of his head...his eye."

"His eye, singular?"

She drew a circle in the air over her own eye. "He has a misshapen iris. I researched it, and the defect is called a coloboma. I had blowups made of my husband's execution video and I had this picture blown up. The man's eye is the same in both. This is the guy."

Mike buried his fingers into his hair, digging them into his scalp. What had this woman put herself through for the past five years? What was she willing to put herself through now?

"I can prove it to you. Let me prove it to you. I have the videos and the stills in a safe deposit box."

He owed her that much, didn't he? He owed Lola Coburn's friend an audience for her manic obsession.

"What is the video you retrieved from Correll's laptop? Who took it? Where was he meeting this man?"

Claire's shoulders dropped as she licked her lips. "It's not DC. Florida, maybe—warm weather, palm trees. I don't know who took the video or why. I don't know why Spencer had it, but I can guess why he trashed it."

"Because it's evidence tying him to this man, whoever he is."

"Exactly."

She wiggled forward in her seat, and a shaft of guilt lanced his chest. He didn't want to give her false hope that he was going along with this insanity, but he had to investigate. He had one last job to do for Prospero, for Jack, and he'd go out doing the best damned job he could, considering his previous assignment was such an abject failure.

"Why would Correll be so careless about the video? Why would he leave it in his trash can?"

She lifted one shoulder. "Maybe he doesn't realize you have to empty your trash can on the computer."

He snorted.

"Don't laugh. Like my mom, Spencer didn't grow up using computers. I'm sure his assistants do a lot of his work on the computer for him. You don't think he actually posts those messages to reach the youth vote on social media platforms himself, do you?"

"How'd you get into his laptop? You told me earlier that you were trying to access his computer last night before the bomb blast."

"That was his desktop at the house. He has a laptop that he keeps with him. I know the password to the laptop and I was able to get to it one night when he was…otherwise engaged."

"Does he keep confidential information on this laptop?" He waved off Betsy Ross as she hovered with the coffeepot.

"No. Personal emails and games mostly, nothing work-related. I don't know how that video got on there, but the minute I saw it, I knew Spencer was up to his eyeballs in something."

He swirled the coffee in his cup, eyeing the mini whirlpool that mimicked his thoughts.

"You don't believe me."

He raised his eyes to hers. "It's a fantastic set of circumstances."

"I know that."

"Does anyone else know about your…suspicions?"

"No." She twirled a lock of blond hair around her finger. "You don't think I realize how crazy this all sounds? That's why I called Lola."

"Lola's an old friend of yours from when you and your mother lived in Florida, right?"

"Yes. We lived there after my father died, with Mom's second husband."

"Correll sits on the Security Council. He must at least know about Jack Coburn even if he's never met him. Does he realize that you're friends with Coburn's wife?" He steepled his fingers and peered at her over the tips.

"No. Like I mentioned before, he and my mother married when I was in my late teens. Lola and I didn't see each other for a while. She was busy with medical school on the East Coast, and I had gone to college at Stanford on the West Coast."

"How do you know he hasn't done some kind of background on you?"

She spread her hands on the table, the three rings on her fingers sparkling in the light from the window. "I don't know, but he has no clue I suspect him of being in bed with terrorists. He realized I was suspicious about Mom's death— that's it, and he thinks I've dropped that train of thought."

Her jaw hardened, and he almost felt a twinge of pity for Senator Spencer Correll. Claire Chadwick would never relinquish her vendetta against her stepfather.

Clasping the back of his neck, he massaged the tight muscles on either side. "Can you show me the videos today?"

"They're at a bank in Maryland."

"Why didn't you take me there right away?"

"I wanted to feel you out first. I wanted to see if I could trust you."

"Why wouldn't you be able to trust me? Lola's husband sent me out here."

She lodged the tip of her tongue in the corner of her mouth and studied his face, her violet gaze meandering from the top of his head to his chin. "I was waiting for you to jump up and down and call me crazy, or worse, talk to me like a child and humor me."

"And?" Her inventory of his face had kindled a slow-burning heat in his belly. If she brought this same level of intensity to bed, she might be the best lay he ever had.

Lola had teased him that her friend's attractiveness would make it difficult for him to concentrate on the job, but he'd shrugged off the warning since a pretty face had never posed a threat to his professionalism before.

Until now. The combined effect of Claire's beauty, sympathetic story, passion and those eyes created a combustible mix that had hit him like a thunderbolt.

He cleared his throat and repeated his question. "And?"

"And you didn't do either one of those things. You don't believe me and you do feel pity for me, but you're a man of honor and you're here to do a job." She leveled a finger at him. "I respect that."

He ran a hand across his stubble, wishing he'd shaved this morning and wondering where he'd misplaced his poker face. Did she just nail that, or what?

"I want to see those videos." He dug his hand into his pocket and pulled out a five-dollar bill, dropping it on the table. "How long is the drive?"

"Less than forty-five minutes."

"Do we have a way to watch the videos?" He stood up and flicked two more dollars on the table.

"I have a laptop in the back of the car."

He ushered her outside and flipped up the collar of his jacket against the cold air. He welcomed its bite, which seemed to wake him up from a dream state. He threw a sideways glance at Claire in the hopes that the chilly slap had made her come to her senses.

She charged across the parking lot with more purpose to her gait than when they'd arrived.

He opened the passenger door of the car. "Unless you want to get your laptop out of the trunk."

"I'll wait." She shrugged out of her coat and tossed it in the back before sliding onto the seat.

He settled behind the wheel. "Can you enter the bank's address in the GPS?"

"I'll give you directions verbally. I'm very careful about what I enter into my GPS."

He raised his eyebrows before starting the car. "You said you weren't on Correll's radar."

"For his terrorist ties, but he knows I've been snooping around his finances."

Rolling his eyes, he said, "There are so many threads here, I can't keep track."

She laughed and then snapped her fingers in front of his face. "Stay with me here, Mike."

"You can laugh?" He pulled away from the parking lot.

"If you can't laugh, you don't stand a chance in life. I still have a son to raise who doesn't have a father."

"You're definitely putting him on a plane to Colorado tomorrow?"

"He needs to see his grandparents. Shane had brothers and sisters and nieces and nephews, so Ethan will have a big family around him. Besides, I need to get him away from you."

"Ouch." He flexed his fingers. "I don't have kids myself, but I always thought I was pretty good with them. I even coach some youth basketball."

She touched his arm. "I'm sorry. That didn't come out right. It's *because* you're so good with Ethan that I want to get him away. Does that make sense?"

"You don't want him getting attached or overhearing the gossip about us." He rolled his shoulders.

"Exactly. I could tell he thought you were something special." She turned her head to look out the window. "You don't have kids?"

"No."

"Ever been married?"

"No."

She jerked her head toward him. "How did that happen?"

He shrugged, all the old familiar excuses curled on his tongue.

Tucking her hair behind her ear, she said, "I suppose your job makes it hard to have a relationship, but even Jack Coburn is happily married with three children."

"Jack has a desk job now, and that desk is at his home."

"You'll be retiring soon. Are you thinking of settling down?"

"With a dog."

"A dog?"

"That's all I can handle."

Her warm laugh had a smile tugging at his lips. Let her think he was joking.

"What kind of dog? Not a little froofy one?"

"Probably a Lab—basic, uncomplicated."

"I didn't know dogs could be complicated." She tapped on the windshield. "You're going to want to take the next exit."

Glancing in his mirror and over his shoulder, he moved to the right. As he took the exit, Claire folded her hands in her lap, revealing two sets of white knuckles.

Her mission always lurked beneath the surface, despite her chatter, smiles and laughter.

Her husband, a journalist kidnapped in Somalia, had died five years ago and her mother had taken a tumble down the stairs a year later. Maybe Claire needed this fiction about her stepfather to keep her from focusing on the primary tragedies. Correll gave her a target for her grief and anger.

He could understand that. He'd had a lot of different targets over the years for his.

They rode in silence for several more miles until they entered the city of Brooktown.

"Are we getting close to the bank?"

"Turn left at the next signal in under a half a mile. It's the Central City Bank. You'll see it on the left after you make the turn."

He turned at the signal and pulled along the curb just past the bank. "Do you want me to go in with you?"

"I don't want anything to seem unusual. I'll just go to my safe deposit box and take the thumb drives."

"You got it." He turned off the ignition and Claire slipped out of the car before the engine stopped.

He'd nabbed a space not too far from the entrance to the bank, and she didn't bother to put on her coat. He watched her tall frame disappear through the glass door, a striking figure in her skin-tight jeans and high boots that came up over the top of her knees.

If he called Jack now, his boss would probably tell him to start his retirement early. Claire's story was too fantastic. It had to be just a coincidence that the CIA director was hit last night—didn't it?

He fiddled with the radio and turned up the classic rock song while drumming his thumbs on the steering wheel. He was about ready to break out his air guitar on the third song in a row when the tap at his window made him grab the steering wheel with both hands.

He glanced out at Claire jerking her thumb toward the rear of the car. He popped the trunk and unlocked the doors.

The car shook as she slammed the trunk of her Lexus. Then she dropped onto the passenger seat, clutching a laptop under one arm. "Got 'em."

"Where are we going to watch? You can't bring them back to the house even if Correll is still in meetings on The Hill."

"Of course not. Hang on a minute." She dipped into her giant bag and pulled out her phone. She tapped the display and started speaking. "How's the party? Is Ethan having fun?"

She cocked her head as she listened, a soft smile playing about her lips. "Don't let him eat too much junk. I'm still packing both of you on a plane tomorrow, stomachache or not."

Mike jabbed her in the ribs. "Tell him not to forget my cupcake."

"Yeah, and Mitchell wants his cupcake." She nodded at him. "Thanks, Lori. See you later."

"Is Ethan bringing me a cupcake?"

"He is." She patted the computer on her lap. "Drive up two blocks to the public library."

Claire had an amazing ability to compartmentalize. It was either a sign of insanity or supreme mental health. "We're going to watch the videos in a public library?"

"The library has small meeting rooms. The schoolkids use them for tutoring but school's out for winter break, so I think they'll be free."

"You seem to know this area well."

"I've used that library for research."

He didn't bother asking her what kind. The woman had tons of money at her disposal and could spend her days playing tennis, going to the spa and lunching with other pampered ladies. Instead she wiled away the hours studying gruesome videos and stalking her stepfather, a US senator.

"Here, here, here."

He slammed on the brakes and jerked the steering wheel to the side to pull up at the curb. "Check that sign. Is it okay to park here?"

"I don't even have to look. Street cleaning tomorrow. We're good."

She hadn't been kidding that she knew the area. He followed her into the library, the large bag hitched over her shoulder with the laptop stashed inside. The musty smell of library books insinuated itself into his consciousness and infused him with a sense of calm. The public library had been one of his refuges, the library and the basketball court.

Claire tugged on the sleeve of his jacket. "This way."

They walked through the stacks, and he trailed his fingers along the spines of the books as if reconnecting with old friends. He read all his books on an electronic device these days, but he missed the feel of a book in his hand.

They passed one glassed-in room where two teenagers hunched over a laptop, giggling.

"Not much work getting done there."

Claire skipped over the next room and then yanked open the door of the following one. "There's free Wi-Fi, too."

"Not that we need it. We're going to be watching the videos from the thumb drives, not posting them on the internet."

"Shane's execution was posted on the internet."

"Still?" Sympathy washed over him as he pulled out a chair for her.

She sank into it with a sigh. "I'm not sure. I haven't searched for it lately."

"Lately?"

Leaning forward, she plugged the laptop into the socket. "I wanted to know where it was so I could keep Ethan away from those websites, block them from our computers."

"Makes sense, but he's a little young."

"I know. That was years ago—when I was obsessed."

He searched her face for any sign of irony, but he saw only concentration as she shoved the first thumb drive into the USB port on the side of the laptop.

She double-clicked on the device and then dragged the lone file to the desktop. "I can bring up the videos side by side. The similarities are more apparent that way."

She pulled out the drive and inserted the second one. She repeated the drag-and-drop action.

As she opened the first video, he held his breath. Before she clicked Play, she double-clicked on the other video.

"Are you ready?"

His heart pounded in his chest and he didn't know why. He'd seen the Shane Chadwick video before, and he'd seen a lot worse. But if he saw nothing in the videos, no likeness between the terrorist who murdered Shane and the man meeting with Correll, he'd have to leave. He'd have to leave Claire Chadwick to her delusions and fantasies.

He didn't want to leave her.

"Mike? Are you ready?"

He scooted his chair closer to the table. "I'm ready. Let's see what you've got here."

She played the first video for a few minutes, stopped it and then played the second. Back and forth she went, freezing the action, pointing out the tilt of the man's head, a hand gesture, the slope of his shoulders, the shape of his face.

She brought up several frames where she'd zoomed in on his eyes, where it looked like the pupil was bleeding into the iris.

It was as if she'd prepared and delivered this presentation many times before. She probably had—in her head.

At the end of the show, she placed her hands on either side of the laptop and drew back her shoulders. "What do you think?"

Had she cast a spell on him with her violet eyes? Had his desire to stay with her, to protect her, colored his perception?

He drew in a deep breath. "I think you're onto something."

She closed her eyes and slumped in her seat. "Thank God. You do see it, don't you?"

"I do. Both men definitely have the same condition with their right eye."

She grabbed his arm. "I'm not crazy, am I? I'm not imagining this?"

He took her slender hand between both of his. "You're not crazy, Claire. He may not be the same man. I mean, it would be quite a coincidence, but there's enough of a similarity between them, especially that coloboma in his eye, to warrant further investigation."

She disentangled her hand from his and, leaning forward, threw her arms around his neck. "You don't know how much that means to me to hear you say that."

Her soft hair brushed the side of his face, a few strands clinging to his lips, and the smell of her musky perfume engulfed him. He dropped one hand to her waist to steady her so she wouldn't topple out of her chair.

A tremble rolled through her body and she pulled away, wiping a tear from her cheek.

"I'm sorry." She sniffled. "I usually don't get emotional like this, but it's been a long time since I could confide in someone."

"I understand, but—" he clicked the mouse twice and closed both videos "—I'm just looking into it at this point. It may lead to nothing."

She dabbed her nose with a tissue and squared her shoulders. "Of course. I didn't mean to put any pressure on you."

He bit the inside of his cheek, drawing blood for his punishment. He should've comforted her, held her, wiped her tears instead of bringing her back to cold, hard reality.

"What's the first step?" She snapped the laptop closed and swept it from the desk.

"I'm going to send those stills and close-ups I copied to your thumb drive to our team at Prospero. I need to get to my secure computer, which I left in the hotel safe."

"We should go back to your hotel anyway, so you can bring the rest of your stuff over to the house." She stuffed the laptop back into her bag.

"Exactly, but I'm keeping the hotel room and I'm leaving a few of my things there."

"Like your secure laptop?"

"Yeah. Speaking of security, I think you should put both thumb drives back in the bank once I complete my transmission."

"Don't worry. I've been guarding those little storage devices with my life." She waved the other thumb drive and zipped it into an inner pocket of the coat she'd flung across the table.

"So," he said as he held up one hand and ticked off his index finger, "we head to my hotel back in DC, I send the images and then we return here to stash everything back in your safe deposit box."

She glanced at her expensive-looking watch. "If we can get back here in time. It's already late."

"Then we'll put both thumb drives in my hotel safe this afternoon, and come back here tomorrow after you drop off Ethan and Lori at the airport." He stood up and stretched, glancing out the window at the rows of stacks. They'd had the laptop with its gruesome images facing away from the window—just another couple of coworkers poring over a project together.

"Sounds like a plan." She shoved out her hand

and then laughed when he took it lightly in his own. "Don't worry, Mike. I'm not going to fall apart again."

He squeezed her hand and pulled her in until they were almost nose to nose. He was close enough to see the flecks in her deep blue eyes that gave them their purple hue. "You have every right and reason to fall apart."

She lifted her shoulders. "Doesn't mean I should."

She broke away from his grasp and spun around to sweep her coat from the table and sling her bag over her shoulder. "Let's get down to business."

He stuffed his arms into his jacket and opened the door for her. The giggling teens had finished whatever it was they were doing, a homeless guy slouched in a chair in the corner and the stacks were empty.

Mike stepped outside behind Claire, and an insistent car alarm assaulted his ears, an unwelcome jolt after the peace and quiet of the library. He stuck his fingers in his ears. "That's so annoying."

"Mike." Claire quickened her pace down the library steps, clamping her bag against her side.

"What? Is that your car?"

"I think it is." She plunged her hand into her coat pocket and aimed the key fob in front of her, pointing it at her car at the curb.

The alarm went silent, but the alarm bells in his head replaced it. "That *was* your car."

"I hope nobody bumped it. I haven't even had it a year."

While Claire inspected her front bumper, Mike trailed around the perimeter of the car. He ran his hand along the driver's side door, skimming his fingers along the windows. "Claire?"

"Yeah?" Her boots clicked as she walked toward him. "Everything looks okay in the front."

"Did you have these scratches on your window like this before?"

She bent forward rubbing her fingers over the grooves in the glass. "No."

"Feel the edge of the door here. Rough, isn't it?"

Her eyebrows collided over her nose as she bent forward and traced a finger along the seam where the window met the door. "It does feel rough. How would that happen?"

His eyes met hers, wide in her pale face. "Someone was trying to use a slim jim to break into your car."

She gasped and shot up to her full height. "Do you think the alarm scared them off? Who would do that in broad daylight on the street?"

"Someone who thought he could make it look like he was just opening the door with a key." His lips formed a thin line and a muscle jumped in his jaw.

"You don't think…?" She flung out one arm. "How would anyone even know we were here? I don't have any business in Brooktown."

He headed toward the trunk, crouched down and poked his head beneath the chassis of her car.

"Mike, what are you doing?"

A few minutes later, his fingers greasy from his exploration, he straightened up and stalked to the front of the car. He dropped to his knees and trailed his fingers along the inside of the wheel well. They tripped over a hard, square object.

"Bingo."

"Bingo? Bingo what?" The slightly hysterical edge to Claire's voice told him she knew what was coming.

He yanked the tracking device from her car and held it up. "Someone's been following you."

Chapter Five

She swayed and braced her hand against the hood of the car. Spencer knew. She'd given herself away somehow. She'd been naive to think a man like Spencer would allow himself to be investigated without turning the tables.

"I—I don't understand. I've been so careful. Why would he have me followed?"

Mike squinted at the tracker and then tossed it in the air. "He doesn't trust you. He probably never forgot that you suspected him of murdering your mother."

"That was almost three years ago. Do you mean to tell me he's been tracking my movements for three years?"

"Maybe. Have you been anywhere, done anything in those three years that would tip him off to anything?"

"Just coming here, where I have no reason to be. I just got the safe deposit box about a year ago."

"So he knows you have a bank account in

Maryland. That's not much." He circled to the front of the car and crouched before it, reaching beneath the body.

"What are you doing? You're not putting it back?"

"If you take it off and throw it in the trash, he's going to know you found it. You shouldn't do anything different." He popped back up and wedged his hip against the hood. "Are you sure it's Correll? Do you have any other enemies?"

"None that I'm aware of." She plucked some tissues from her bag and waved them at him. "Wipe your hands on these."

"No ex-boyfriends stalking you?"

"Are you kidding? I haven't had any boyfriends since…" She shoved the tissues into his hand.

"Then we'll assume it's your stepfather, and all he knows is that you come out to a bank and library in Brooktown a few times a month."

"If you leave that thing on there, he's going to know we went to your hotel in DC."

"So what? I already told him I'd taken a room at the Capitol Plaza and left most of my stuff there." He'd shredded the tissues wiping his hands and then crumpled them into a ball. "Let me get rid of this and we'll satisfy Correll's curiosity by going to my hotel."

She held up her key as he walked back from the trash can near the steps of the library. "Do you still want to drive?"

"Sure." He snatched the dangling keys from her fingers and caught her wrist. "Don't worry. That tracker told him nothing."

She let out the breath trapped in her lungs and nodded. His touch made her feel secure, but she had to be careful. She'd made him uncomfortable with her previous display of emotion. For all his outer friendliness and charm, he had an aloof quality—except when he'd been kissing her last night. He hadn't seemed to mind her touch then.

Of course, the drive for sex came from a completely different place than the trigger for empathy. She'd rather have him desire her than pity her, anyway.

His lashes fell over his dark eyes and he pressed a kiss against the inside of her wrist. Then he dropped her hand. "Let's get going."

She had no idea what emotions had played across her face for him to do that, but she'd have to try to duplicate them sometime soon.

She slipped into the passenger seat of the car, glancing at the scratches on the driver's-side window as Mike opened the door.

When he settled behind the wheel, she turned to him. "If Spencer's lackey had managed to get into my car, then what? What exactly had he been looking for?"

"Your laptop? That video?"

"Spencer couldn't possibly know about the video. I left it in his trash can after I discovered it."

He cranked on the ignition and pulled away from the curb. "He's grasping at straws, just like you. How did you manage to get into Correll's laptop?"

"I bribed his admin assistant, Fiona."

"How do you know she didn't tell him?"

"She wouldn't. She let me have access to his laptop and gave me his password. If she had told him that, he would've gotten get rid of her for sure and changed his password."

"How do you know that wasn't his plan all along? Why'd she do it? Money?"

"I'm not going to lie. Money did exchange hands, but I played on the emotions of a woman scorned."

"Fiona? Scorned?"

She plucked an imaginary piece of fuzz from the arm of her sweater. "Spencer had been having an affair with Fiona. I overheard him making plans with another woman for an afternoon tryst. I figured it was a good time to hightail it to his office and do some snooping, and while I was there I let Spencer's plans for a little afternoon delight drop into Fiona's lap. She was more than happy to cough up his password and let me into his office."

He whistled. "You're pretty good at this cloak-and-dagger stuff. Does Correll have a weakness for the ladies?"

"Oh yeah. I can almost guarantee you that he cheated on my mom."

"That's good."

She jerked her head to the side and he held up one hand. "Not that he cheated on your mother, but that he has a wandering eye. It's a weakness that can be exploited, as you discovered."

"I like how you think, Becker." She shoved her hair behind one ear. "I know you have to continue to analyze the videos before committing yourself or the Prospero resources to investigating any further. I'm not getting ahead of the game here, just so you know."

"I got it."

She lifted her phone from a pocket in her purse. "Excuse me a minute while I check on Ethan. The party should be wrapping up soon, and after finding that device on my car, I honestly can't wait to get my son out of this town."

She got Lori on the phone, but Ethan was too busy with the pony rides to talk. Lori filled her in on all the details, which soothed the twinges of guilt she felt for missing out on spending time with her son.

When he'd received this party invitation earlier in the month, Claire had arranged for Lori to take him, since Lola had told her an agent would be heading her way before Christmas. As much as she loved seeing all the kids having a blast and chatting with the other moms, this day with Mike had proven to be fruitful.

She ended the call and sighed as she cupped the

phone in her hand while Lori sent her a picture of Ethan on the back of a dapple-gray.

"Missing the fun? Sounds like a pretty extravagant party if it includes pony rides."

"Yeah."

She held the phone in front of his face as he idled at a signal.

"Wow. I never went to birthday parties like that."

She traced her finger around Ethan's smiling face. "Every party he's been to at this school, it seems like the parents are trying to one-up each other. I'm not sure that's a very healthy environment for kids. What were your birthday parties like?"

"I only had one birthday party—for my seventh birthday—and there were definitely no ponies there." His mouth twisted. "It ended early when my old man showed up unexpectedly, drunk as a skunk, and started popping all the balloons with a lit cigarette."

"I'm sorry. That doesn't sound like much fun."

"That was my old man—life of his own party." He dropped his shoulders, which he'd raised stiffly to his ears.

He pointed to the phone in her lap. "You must've had parties like that."

"I did."

"And you turned out okay."

"Did I?"

"Well, we've established you're not crazy."

"Did we?"

"Even if the guys in the videos aren't the same person, you have several good reasons to believe they are."

Leaning her head against the cold glass of the window, she stared at the landscape whizzing by. "It's good to have someone on my side."

"I tend to be a loner, but having backup is always good."

Claire thumbed through a few text messages on her phone, her mind on the man next to her. He reminded her of a chameleon. He could be the charming fiancé, the kid-friendly visitor, the no-nonsense spy. Would she ever get to truly know him?

She stole a glance at him sideways through her lashes, taking in the strong hands that gripped the steering wheel and the hard line of his jaw. Without a wife, without children, what did he plan to do in his retirement years? He was too young to sit on some pier fishing or to stroll along some golf course.

"My hotel is coming up. We'll retrieve my computer from the safe, send the video stills and lock it back up along with your thumb drives."

"Then when we get back to the house, we act as if everything's normal and that we never found a tracker on the car."

"And we don't lie about our whereabouts."

She covered her mouth with her hand. "Depending on how long that tracker's been attached to my car, it's already too late for that. I've never admitted going to Brooktown, but he's going to know I've been there."

"So what? He doesn't know what you're doing there and it's really none of his business, is it?"

"None at all." She tilted her chin toward a glittering high-rise hotel. "Isn't that it?"

"Yeah, I'm hoping to find a spot in the short-term parking out front so I don't have to leave the car with a valet."

He pulled into the circular drive in front of the hotel and slid into the last available parking space in the small lot to the right of the main building.

He guided her up to his room and ushered her in first.

"Nice." She took a turn around the suite.

"Only the best for Mitchell Brown. He's supposed to be a successful businessman. Do you think Correll will be checking me out?"

"Two hours ago, I would've said no. He doesn't care who I marry since my marriage isn't going to take anything out of his pocket." She perched on the edge of a chair by the window. "After finding the tracking device? My bet is he's going to look up Mitchell Brown to make sure he's no threat. Will he be?"

"Mitch? Nah. He works for an international conglomerate that makes plastic coffee-cup lids, stir sticks and sleeves. Grew up in Chicago, went right to work in sales." He yanked open the closet doors and dropped to his knees in front of the safe.

"Where did we meet, sweetheart?"

He cranked his head over his shoulder and she fluttered her eyelashes at him.

"We should've had this discussion last night. In fact, I was planning on it until that car bomb exploded." He turned back to the safe and punched in some numbers.

"It's a good thing Spencer didn't ask this morning. I think Ethan's presence at the breakfast table saved us." She crossed one leg over the other and tapped her toe. "So, where did we? Meet, I mean."

"Don't you remember? It was that fund-raiser for the girls' school in Yemen. My company committed a million bucks to the cause."

"Was it love at first sight?"

"For me, it was." He held up his laptop and crossed the room to place it on the table next to her. "That's why I fell so fast."

"And you were so different from anyone else I'd ever known—politically obtuse, culturally challenged, a breath of fresh air."

He chuckled as he fired up the laptop. "Don't get too carried away."

He turned the computer away from her as he tapped on the keys, probably entering passwords. Then he inserted the thumb drive, waited and continued clicking away.

Blowing out a breath, he powered down the laptop. "All done. Let's see if Prospero can get a line on this guy. It's not like agencies besides ours haven't tried to discover the identity of your husband's executioner. The English accent alone has puzzled us for years, and I'm sure others have noticed the eye, but they've never gotten another possible look at him—until now."

"So, we wait?"

"The least exciting aspect of my job." He held out his hand. "The other drive? I'll put every-thing in this safe since it's too late to return to Brooktown, and I'm sure you want to see Ethan when he gets home from the party…and I want my cupcake."

"Don't hold your breath." She dropped the thumb drive into his cupped palm. "He's five. He tends to forget anything that doesn't relate to his immediate happiness."

"Ah, to be five again." He placed the items in the safe and locked it. "Do you want to watch the news for a while before we go back? I haven't seen any coverage on the director's murder since I tuned in to the morning news shows."

"Are you going to tell Jack what we saw last night? The valet placing the device beneath the car and running off?"

"I already told him, but that story is out any-way. There were a couple of other witnesses who got a better look at the man than we did."

"I'm sure he's a low-level guy who'll never talk even if they find him. He's not going to be implicating Spencer or anyone else."

"Maybe." He aimed the remote at the TV. "It remains to be seen how much Prospero will be involved in the investigation. We come into play once the person has been identified, except…"

"Except what?" She averted her gaze from the images shifting across the TV screen—Jerry Haywood's life in review.

"We've been tracking a…situation for the past four months, one that involves the assassination of high-level officials, but these hits have all been on foreigners so far."

"This might be related." She rose from the chair and took a turn around the room.

"Anything is possible."

"That means Spencer was involved with those other murders, because there is no doubt in my mind he's responsible for what happened last night."

"Slow down." He turned up the volume on the TV. "We wait."

While Mike soaked up the news of the day, she retreated to the bathroom, washed her hands and splashed some water on her face. She returned to the room to find Mike sprawled across the sofa, his long legs hanging off the edge.

"Anything new?"

"The talking heads have nothing, but while I

was listening to my stomach growl it occurred to me that you haven't eaten anything today. I, at least, had a big breakfast." He shook a finger at her. "You can't run with the big boys on a couple cups of coffee."

She placed a hand on her stomach. "I forgot all about food."

His gaze raked her from head to toe. "That happen a lot?"

"Are you implying I'm skinny?"

"You look like one of those high-fashion models who wear the weird clothes—not that you're wearing weird clothes—and eat two olives a day."

"My mom was a model. I inherited her build."

"Yeah, yeah, well, you're not a model, so you can actually eat more than two olives a day." He turned off the TV. "The restaurant downstairs isn't bad. Do you want to grab a sandwich before we return to the scene of the crime?"

"We're about fifteen minutes away from my house. There's plenty to eat there." Narrowing her eyes, she wedged a hand on her hip. "Are you putting off going back there for some reason?"

"For some reason? Let's see, I have to pretend I'm engaged, have to pretend I'm someone else, my boss's boss was just murdered there." He stood up and stretched. "Seems to me I have a lot of reasons."

"Sounds like a whole bunch of whining to me. Besides, what is all that compared to a cupcake?"

"You have a point there."

When they arrived back at the house, everything looked normal—except for the yellow tape that still fluttered in the crisp breeze, the men and women in dark suits and dark glasses milling around, and the press hovering like a bunch of vultures across the street. Completely normal.

The security detail in front of the house waved them through, and they ducked into the house. Claire tilted her head back to take in the towering Christmas tree at the end of the foyer, which had been restored to last night's glory.

Mike whistled. "The Christmas tree is redecorated and all of the windows have already been replaced. Your stepfather must've had an army out here."

"It took an army." Spencer jogged down the staircase. "I hope you two had a good day and were able to set this all aside."

"We did." Claire hooked her arm through Mike's. "Any leads? Did the FBI find the valet yet?"

"Nothing yet, although they're splashing a composite of him all over the news. You haven't seen it yet?" Spencer placed a well-manicured hand on the curved balustrade at the bottom of the staircase. "Where did you go today?"

Mike pressed his shoulder against hers. "We drove down to Mount Vernon and then to a very special place in Maryland."

She stiffened, but plastered a smile on her face and nodded.

"What's so special about Maryland?" Spencer cocked his head, but the smile on his lips didn't reach his eyes.

"Oh, Mitch." She tapped his arm. "I thought that was supposed to be our secret."

"Now I'm really intrigued." Spencer leaned against the banister as if he had all day to listen, and panic flared in her chest.

Mike ran a hand through his dark hair. "Claire and I communicated a lot face-to-face through our laptops, and I proposed to her while she was in Maryland. I wanted to visit the exact spot in person."

"Modern technology. I'm glad I'm not dating these days." Spencer winked.

Claire gritted her teeth behind her smile. He didn't have to date. He just bedded half the women who worked for him.

"Are Lori and Ethan home from the party yet?"

Spencer raised his eyes to the ceiling. "I was just upstairs getting a detailed account. Lori's getting him all packed up for tomorrow—that is, if you still want him going out to the Chadwicks'."

"Don't you think it's even more important now after what happened last night?"

"I don't think anyone here is in danger. Some

terrorist organization targeted the director and was successful. We're not expecting any more hits."

Because you got what you wanted?

"You sound so confident." Claire hugged herself. "I'm not so sure about that. Has anyone taken credit yet? Director Haywood's assassination was a huge coup. I can't imagine the people responsible won't want to crow about it."

Spencer reached out and patted her shoulder, and she tried hard not to recoil. "Don't concern yourself with it, Claire. You don't want to go down that road again, do you?"

Her nostrils flared and her palm tingled with the urge to slap his smug face.

As if sensing her urge, Mike took her hand and circled his thumb on her palm. "Claire's just asking normal questions. I think we all wait for the other shoe to drop when something like this happens."

"Since you two are engaged, I'm sure Claire told you about her…troubles." Spencer touched her cheek with the smooth tip of his middle finger. "She's worked hard to come back from those dark days, but she's still a little shaky."

Claire reared back from him, hot rage thumping through her veins. "I am not…shaky."

Mike put his arm around her shoulders and brushed past Spencer still perched on the bottom step. "Claire's fine. We're going to check on Ethan."

She preceded Mike up the staircase, her body trembling with anger. When they got to the second-floor landing, she grabbed his hand and pulled him into the library.

She shut the door behind them and leaned against it, her eyes closed, her breath coming out in short spurts. "Bastard!"

Mike took her by the shoulders. "Don't let him get to you."

Her eyes flew open at the same time they flooded with tears. "You know what he's talking about, don't you? You, Prospero, would've checked me out thoroughly before taking this assignment."

Pulling her close, he whispered in her ear, "Anyone would've had a breakdown, Claire. He's a jerk for bringing it up, especially when you're asking honest questions, but we already know that."

"Y-you know he had me committed? They took Ethan away from me."

His arms tightened around her and she melted against his solid chest, allowing herself a moment of weakness. He rested his cheek against the top of her head. "It must've been tough, but I don't think anyone who knew your situation would think you're crazy. What you discovered on those two videos has real merit."

She pressed her nose against his shirt and

sniffled. "I'm sorry. That's twice today I got weepy and used you as a tissue."

Smiling a crooked smile, he looked down into her eyes. "I don't mind. I've been used in worse ways."

She quirked an eyebrow at him and he laughed. "Wait. That didn't come out right."

"Okay, let's go see Ethan." She took a long, shuddering breath.

They hesitated outside Ethan's door, which had been left open a crack, and Claire practiced her brightest smile.

Mike nodded and gave her a thumbs-up.

She scooped in a breath before pushing open the door. If she did have another breakdown, at least she had the right man on hand to catch her.

Chapter Six

The following morning Mike jogged downstairs, leaving Claire in Ethan's bedroom. Mother and son should have some alone time before the boy left for the holidays. Claire hoped to be able to join Ethan in Colorado for Christmas, and maybe that was where she belonged, away from this craziness.

If Prospero came back with any kind of match between the two men in the video, the agents could handle it from there. Claire needed a break from all this, and maybe once he retired he could do a little skiing in Colorado. That wouldn't be too obvious, would it? He'd already kind of bonded with Ethan last night over that cupcake.

He pushed through the dining room doors and Correll popped up from where he'd been...hovering over Lori Seaver, Ethan's nanny.

"Good morning." He pulled out a chair across from the two of them as a quick blush stained Lori's cheeks. Had Correll been putting moves on the nanny?

"Just giving Lori some skiing tips. Do you ski, Mitch?"

"I do, took it up as an adult." In fact, skiing and snowboarding had been part of his training with Prospero. His family could've never afforded a sport like skiing. Hell, his family couldn't have afforded sending him downhill in an inner tube.

"So did I." Correll pushed off the table where he'd been parked next to Lori and tapped his nose. "I think you and I are alike in a lot of ways, Mitch."

Mitch swallowed a mouthful of coffee too fast and burned the roof of his mouth, but he kept a straight face. "Poor boy making it good?"

"Something like that." Correll narrowed his dark eyes as he studied Mike.

God, the man thought he was marrying Claire for her money. Maybe that wasn't such a bad cover story.

Liz, the maid from yesterday, came in from the kitchen bearing a plate of food. Couldn't these people get their own damned food? He and Correll were nothing alike since it seemed the senator had adapted easily to being waited on by the minions that kept his life running like a well-oiled machine.

"I remember what you liked from yesterday, Mr. Brown."

"Thanks, Liz. After that dinner Jerome made last night, I'm not sure I'm up for a full breakfast."

She put the plate down in front of him, over-flowing with eggs, bacon and home fries. A basket of Jerome's biscuits were already steaming on the table. "Give it a try."

When Liz disappeared back into the kitchen, Correll chuckled. "You'll get used to it, Mitch."

"Sir?"

"Getting waited on." He winked. "You might even learn to enjoy it."

Had the man been reading his mind?

The doorbell chimed deep within the house and Lori jerked her head up.

Correll patted her hand. "You still nervous, too? You and my stepdaughter need to learn to relax."

Mike concentrated on his plate and stabbed a blob of scrambled egg. Correll had a very odd attitude toward an obvious terrorist attack in front of his own place of residence.

He seemed to be expecting the visitor as he excused himself and left the room.

Mike swallowed and took a sip of coffee. "Are you looking forward to the trip? That must be a nice perk working for a family like this."

"It is, but Claire isn't one to take her son all over the world. I think she'd planned to raise him in Florida...before she decided to get involved in the investigation of her husband's murder. Then when she...well, had some problems, she ended up staying here."

"Were you here when Claire had her problems?" Lori's brown eyes rounded, taking up half of her heart-shaped face.

"Oh, no. When Claire got better, she wouldn't have that woman—Andrea—anywhere near Ethan."

Any more probing came to an end when Correll entered the dining room again with two men in suits following him.

Not that Mike wanted to go behind Claire's back and question Lori about her breakdown. If he had questions, he'd ask Claire straight-up.

Correll gestured to the suits. "These men are from the FBI, and they'd like to talk to Claire before she takes Ethan to the airport. Do you want to get her?"

"Sure." He glanced at the older man. "I'm assuming this is about what happened the other night."

The older agent adjusted his glasses while the younger one answered. "It is, and you are?"

Mike thrust out his hand. "Mitchell Brown, Ms. Chadwick's fiancé."

He shook hands with both agents, confident that his cover would stick even with the FBI. "I'll get Claire."

Lori got up from the table. "I'll come with you to stay with Ethan."

Mike took the stairs two at a time, leaving Lori in his dust. He tapped on Ethan's door as he pushed it open.

Two faces looked up from the bed where Claire had Ethan in her lap with a book in front of them.

"Hate to interrupt your story, but a couple of men are downstairs and want to talk to you."

"Really?" Claire tossed her blond hair over one shoulder. "What kind of men?"

"I'll tell you on the way downstairs."

As Claire slid off the bed, Lori joined them. "I'll keep an eye on Ethan, Claire. Is he ready to go?"

"Yes, are you?"

"All packed."

Claire handed her a book with a bull sitting in a field of flowers on the cover. "We're right in the middle."

"I'll finish reading the story for you, Ethan." Lori took Claire's place on the bed.

When they were in the hallway, Mike shut Ethan's door. "They're two FBI agents."

"About the car bomb?"

"That's what they said."

She put her hand on his arm and lowered her voice. "Are we not admitting we were witnesses?"

"Nothing to be gained by it at this point, and I don't want to draw attention to myself."

"Got it." She squared her shoulders and walked downstairs, graceful on a pair of high-heeled boots, her slim hips swaying hypnotically.

He blinked and shook his head. *Snap out of it, Becker.*

When they reached the bottom of the staircase, the agents were waiting for them.

They introduced themselves to Claire as Agents Finnegan and Glotz.

Glotz, the younger agent, asked, "Is there someplace we can talk privately, Mrs. Chadwick? Senator Correll suggested the small office off the foyer."

"Since that's my office, that'll work. You don't mind if my fiancé joins us, do you?"

The agents exchanged a glance that made the hair on the back of his neck quiver.

"No."

Claire swung open the door and ushered them all inside the small, feminine office. The seat in the bay window sported rose-colored cushions, and Mike sat in a chair with such spindly legs, he had a feeling that it would collapse beneath him at any moment.

The agents in the chairs facing Claire's ornate desk must've felt the same way, as they perched on the edges of their seats.

Claire folded her hands in front of her, the rings on her fingers sparkling beneath the desk lamp. "What can I help you with?"

Glotz placed a folder on the desk, flipped it open and positioned a photograph in front of Claire. "Do you recognize this man, Mrs. Chadwick?"

Mike craned his neck over the shoulders of the

agents but only got a glimpse of a young, dark-skinned man.

"It's Ms. Chadwick, and yes, I do recognize him. And you know I recognize him or you wouldn't be uncomfortably shifting in those Louis Quinze chairs staring at me."

Mike gulped, his stomach twisting into a knot. Had Claire been keeping secrets from him?

Glotz tapped the picture. "Can you tell us who he is, Ms. Chadwick?"

She snorted. "You know who he is. The question is, why are you asking me about him?"

Agent Finnegan hunched forward in his chair, his face red up to the line of his gray hair. "Tell us his name, Ms. Chadwick."

Mike cleared his throat. "Claire?"

She held up a hand. "It's okay, Mitch. This man is Hamid Khan."

"And you've been in contact with him?" Glotz's calm tone contrasted with his partner's aggressive one.

Good cop, bad cop, but why were they playing this game with Claire?

"Lately? Have I been in contact with him lately? No."

"You've contacted him before." Finnegan jabbed a stubby finger in Claire's direction.

"Agent Finnegan..." Mike half rose from his chair, his hands curling into fists.

Glotz cast an apologetic half smile in his direction. "We don't have a problem with your presence, Mr. Brown, but please don't interfere with our questioning."

Mike spluttered. He could be a protective fiancé, but not someone overly knowledgeable about FBI procedures. "Does Claire need a lawyer? I don't like this questioning."

"I'm fine, babe." She picked up the picture with both hands. "I contacted Hamid when I was looking into my husband's execution at the hands of terrorists. Why are you asking me about him now?"

"Hamid Khan was the man posing as a valet parking attendant at your party the other night. We have a composite sketch from witnesses."

Claire dropped the picture, and Mike sat up in his chair to try to get a look at the man again. He didn't know any Hamid Khan, but why in the hell had Claire been in contact with terrorists?

She recovered herself and folded her hands on top of the photo. "That's impossible. I had been in touch with Hamid because of his uncle, but Hamid was no extremist. He was studying to be an engineer and wanted no part of his uncle's radicalism. I was able to get him into the US on a student visa, but that's as far as it went."

Finnegan pinched the picture between the tips of his blunt fingers and slid it from beneath Claire's hands. "Maybe then, but this is now."

"I don't believe it for a minute. I would've..."

She stopped and huffed out a breath. "I would've known if he was someone capable of this—he wasn't."

Mike's muscles tensed. She was going to spill the beans about seeing the valet from the library window. These guys would've been even more suspicious than they were now if they discovered she'd lied about seeing anything from that window.

Glotz slid the photo from his partner's possession and put it back in the folder. "You're not going anywhere in the near future, are you, Ms. Chadwick?"

"No."

"If we—" Glotz steepled his fingers "—came back with a search warrant for any computers you own, that wouldn't be a problem, would it?"

The color on her cheeks heightened and her long lashes fluttered for a second. "No."

"Very good." Glotz placed his hands on the desk and pushed up from the chair, still mindful that his ass had been planted on a chair that cost more than he'd see in one year's salary.

Finnegan stood up with much less grace and hunched over the desk. "Thanks for your cooperation, Mrs. Chadwick. If we need anything else, we'll let you know."

With the questioning over, Finnegan had reverted back to his gruff but civil self.

Mike hurried to the office door and swung it

open. The tail end of Correll's suit jacket disappeared around the corner of the foyer. Had he been listening at the keyhole?

"Gentlemen, if there's nothing else, we'll see you out. Claire and I need to take her son to the airport."

A maid appeared on silent feet with the agents' coats.

"Just don't hop on any planes yourself, Mrs. Chadwick." Finnegan hunched into his overcoat and saluted.

When the front door closed behind them, Claire sighed. "What they're saying isn't true."

Mike shook his head as Correll came into view from the corner behind her.

"What the hell was that all about, Claire?"

"The FBI thinks they have the valet. It's someone I was in contact with after Shane's murder." She flicked her fingers in the air. "It's all garbage anyway. We need to get Lori and Ethan to the airport. Mitch and I will probably be out the rest of the day."

"Be careful out there, Claire. Those two agents seemed pretty serious. I knew the time you spent looking into Shane's death would come back to haunt you."

She started up the stairs and glanced over her shoulder. "It's not haunting me."

Correll shrugged his shoulders and gave Mike a pitying look. "She's your problem now."

ONE HOUR AND one tear-filled goodbye later, Mike accelerated out of the airport with Claire sniffling beside him.

"He looked so grown-up with his little back-pack." She clutched his arm. "He didn't look scared, did he?"

"I haven't known your son that long, and I'm no expert on little kids, but I don't think a smile from ear to ear and hopping from one foot to the other on the escalator signals fear for a five-year-old boy."

She dabbed her eyes and then waved the tissue in the air. "I don't want him to feel sad, exactly, but a little longer hug would've been nice."

"It probably won't hit him until he's at his grandparents' in the middle of the night and realizes he can't run into your bed whenever he wants."

Her hand returned to his arm. "I hope he's not going to be scared."

"You said he had lots of cousins out there for the holidays?"

"Yes, tons."

"He'll be fine. Everything's always better when you have kids your own age around."

"Did you?"

He fumbled for his sunglasses in the cup holder. "Only child here. I almost had a younger sibling once, but my mother lost the baby after a partic-

ularly bad beating at the hands of my father. She
never tried again."

Claire pressed a hand to her mouth. "I'm so
sorry, Mike. Did your mother ever leave your father?"

"Not until the day she died in a car accident—
his fault. He was driving drunk and they were
fighting. He crossed the median and wrapped his
car around a lamppost. The wrong person died in
that accident."

"H-how old were you when that happened?"

"Seventeen." He ran a hand over his mouth.
"I almost killed the bastard, but my basketball
coach got to me first. My dad went to prison, and
I lived the rest of my senior year of high school
at Coach's house and enlisted in the marines the
day I graduated."

The gentle pressure of her hand on his thigh
brought him back to the present. "I'm sorry. That
sure as hell falls into the too-much-information
category."

She didn't answer except to give his leg a gentle squeeze.

Why had he spilled his guts like that? If he
didn't watch it, he'd be blabbing about his worry
that witnessing all that violence as a child had
ruined him for any kind of relationship. She was
already worried about her own mental health; she
didn't need to start worrying about his.

"So, what's the plan? My hotel first to pick up

the drives, check on a response from Prospero and then head to the bank to secure the drives in your safe deposit box?"

"Sounds good."

He rolled his shoulders to relieve the tightness that had bunched his muscles when he'd revealed his sob story to Claire. He needed to get this ball back into her court.

"Do you have anything else to tell me about this Hamid Khan? I don't think he's on Prospero's radar at all."

"Why would he be? Except for the connection to his uncle, he's not an extremist."

"Who's his uncle?"

"Tamar Aziz. Are you familiar with him?"

"Yeah, low-level guy, a driver, bodyguard type."

"That's right, but he's in the thick of things, and that's not Hamid."

"How'd you get in contact with Hamid?"

"Through some different channels. I got some leads from Shane's interpreter. He'd been kidnapped along with Shane, but he was released."

"You play dangerous games, Claire—then and now."

"Maybe so, but Hamid was never a danger, and as you may have gathered, I almost blurted out that the valet I saw near the director's car was most definitely not Hamid." She swept the hair back from her face. "They're getting bad information from someone."

"I wonder how the FBI came up with his name. They must've been looking into his activities thoroughly to come across your connection to him."

"If they are, they're allowing the real perpetrators to escape."

"The real perpetrators who are somehow connected to your stepfather?"

"Exactly."

"So your stepfather must've been thrilled to see the FBI show up on his doorstep and question you about Hamid Khan." He reached out and dialed down the heat. He was starting to sweat under his layers of clothes—or maybe it was the subject matter.

She tapped the edge of her phone against her chin. "Are you implying that Spencer himself somehow implicated Hamid?"

"He knew you'd been contacting players. It's no stretch to believe he knew their names."

Hunching her shoulders, she crossed her arms. "He's probably been spying on me ever since he couldn't have me committed for life."

"And you've been spying on him. What a game of cat and mouse."

"He's going to think we're a couple of sentimental fools coming back out to Brooktown." She turned to face him, a smile playing about her lips. "How did you come up with that story, anyway? You proposed to me online? That's romantic."

"Hey." He smacked the steering wheel before

pulling into the hotel's circular drive. "I wanted to see the very spot where you were sitting when I popped the question. That's romantic."

"If you say so." She rolled her eyes.

He pulled up behind a car and stuck his head out the window, yelling at the valet. "Is it okay if I leave my car here for about fifteen minutes?"

"Sure. Do you mind leaving the keys in case we have to move it?"

He killed the engine and dangled the keys out the window in exchange for a red ticket, which he dropped into the pocket of his shirt.

The valet opened Claire's door and she paused. "Do you think it might take longer than fifteen minutes if you've gotten a response?"

"I don't expect any feedback this soon. Besides, they have your car keys if they have to move the car."

With no response from Prospero, it took them less than fifteen minutes to gather his laptop and Claire's thumb drives from the safe.

He hauled a small carry-on bag onto the bed. "I might as well stuff the rest of my clothes in here and take them back to your place."

She pointed as his computer. "And the laptop? Do you think it'll be safe at my house with Spencer there?"

"Why would Correll want to poke around my laptop?"

"You never know."

"Don't worry. It's as secure as Fort Knox, and I want to have it with me in case Prospero comes through with something today."

He slipped his laptop into a separate case and then wedged the case on top of his wheeled bag. "You all set?"

"Yes. It's not like I don't trust the hotel safe, but I'll feel a lot better when these are back in my safe deposit box." She patted her bag where she'd stashed the drives.

"Onward to Maryland, then."

On the drive east, they kept the conversation light—no abusive fathers, no nervous breakdowns, no terrorists. This was what he looked forward to in retirement. He'd never pictured a woman by his side before, but Claire's presence felt right, felt good.

By the time they reached the bank, he felt as if they were on a date—the small talk, the mutual discovery of the petty likes and dislikes that comprised a person, the palpable sexual tension that buzzed between them.

In fact, he hadn't had such a successful first date in a long time—or maybe ever.

WHEN THE BANK came into view, Claire's stomach sank. For a short time with Mike in the car, she'd felt almost normal.

She liked him, everything about him. Why did she ever think he was standoffish? He'd revealed quite a bit about himself today. The story about his abusive father had her heart hurting for the pain Mike must've endured as a child.

Ethan would grow up without a father, but she'd make damned sure she'd surround him with love. Who knew? Maybe one day she'd meet a man good enough to be Ethan's dad.

Mike parked her car at the curb about half a block down from the bank. "I'll wait in the car."

"I won't be long—in and out." She grabbed her coat from the backseat and put it on while standing on the sidewalk. Then she waved to Mike and slammed the car door.

Entering the bank, she veered toward the end of the teller windows and stopped in front of Dorothy's desk. Dorothy looked up from a computer screen, where she was helping a teller. "Be right there, Claire."

Two minutes later, Dorothy's heels clicked on the floor as she approached her desk. She opened her drawer and withdrew a key chain, and then buzzed the security door for Claire.

Claire joined Dorothy on the other side of the door and followed her down a short hallway to the safe deposit area. Dorothy used her key along with a code to open the main door of the safe. They both stepped through the door, and rows and rows of metal boxes stretched out on either side of Claire.

"Twenty-two sixty-one, right?" Dorothy moved

to the left and bent forward to insert her key into Claire's box.

"You have a good memory, Dorothy."

"Well, I did just open it earlier today."

Claire nodded and smiled as Dorothy backed out of the room. Maybe Dorothy's memory wasn't that great. Claire had been here yesterday, not this morning. She inserted her own key into the second lock on the box and slid it out of its cavity.

She turned and placed it on the table that ran the length of the small room. She reached into her purse, her fingers searching for the two drives. Curling her hand around both at once, she pulled them out.

She lifted the lid on the box and froze. Licking her lips, she tilted her head to check the number on the box and then glanced to her left to squint at the number on the empty slot.

With her heart pounding, she plucked the first stack of bills, neatly bound, from her box and ran her thumb along the edge.

Where had this come from? Even though she knew she was alone in the room, she looked around as if expecting to find an answer from the tight-lipped safe deposit boxes guarding their own secrets.

She dropped the packet of money on the table and picked up the second stack of bills, again neatly bound. Four more bundles nestled in the safe deposit box, giving her a total of six.

How could the bank make a mistake like this? She was the only person with the other key. She didn't want to leave the bills in her box. She'd better bring them out to Dorothy.

She dumped the money onto the table and scanned the room for a bag. Of course, the bank didn't just leave those lying around, and she couldn't walk into the main area clutching the cash in her hands.

Her big bag gaped open on the table, and she started stuffing the stacks inside. She left her box open on the table and hugged her purse to her chest as she walked out of the safe deposit box room. The door slammed behind her as it was designed to do.

She exited the door to the main area of the bank and turned toward Dorothy's desk. That was when she saw them.

A man and a woman in dark suits were talking to Dorothy, whose eyes were bugging out of her face. They bugged out even farther when she caught sight of Claire. Dorothy pointed at her and the man and woman turned in unison.

A chill zipped down her spine and her step faltered.

The two feds pivoted toward her, the female reaching inside her jacket.

A flood of adrenaline surged through her. She clasped the purse tighter, wrapping her arms around the money and the two thumb drives still inside. Her long stride got longer. She put her head down and made a beeline for the door.

"Ms. Chadwick," the woman called behind her.

Claire shoved through the glass doors and took off down the sidewalk toward the car. Mike must've seen her in the rearview mirror because the engine growled to life at her approach.

"Ms. Chadwick, stop." This time it was the male who yelled after her, but she had no intention of stopping for him, either.

Despite her high-heeled boots, she took off in a run, extending her hand in readiness for the door handle. When her fingers tucked around the cold metal of the handle, she could hear the flurry of someone sprinting behind her.

She tugged open the door and scrambled inside the car. The man had caught up with her and made a grab for her coat as it flew out behind her.

"Claire?" Mike's voice gave her strength and purpose.

"Go, Mike! Just go!"

That was all he needed from her. No questions, no answers.

He floored the gas pedal and the car lurched away from the curb, flinging the door open and shedding the government man hanging on to it.

Chapter Seven

The familiar streets of Brooktown passed by in a blur. Mike had slowed the car down a few blocks past the bank to give Claire a chance to close the door and loosen her death grip on the seat.

Now only their heavy breathing filled the silence between them as Mike maneuvered through the streets at high speed. His gaze darted between his rearview and side mirrors, and then he suddenly screeched to a stop before the bridge.

He charged out of the car, disappeared in the front and then popped up holding the tracking device.

He stepped away from the car and chucked the device into the water. Then they sped across the bridge.

After another five miles or so, he balanced his palms on top of the steering wheel and flexed his fingers. "What happened back there?"

"I opened my safe deposit box to put the drives back and found this." She unzipped her bag, plunged her hand inside and withdrew the packets of neatly stacked bills. "Money."

Mike swore. "How much is it?"

"I didn't stop to count it, but there are six stacks of varying denominations."

"So, your natural response was to stuff the cash in your bag and run from the FBI?"

She jerked her head around. "I was scared. How do I know those two aren't working for Spencer?"

"We don't know anything at this point. I saw them enter the bank, and it gave me pause. In fact, it set off low-level alarm bells in my head."

"Exactly." She formed her fingers into a gun and pointed at him. "When I discovered the money, I freaked out. How could a bank make a mistake like that? I didn't want to leave the stacks in there for one minute and there were no bags in the room, so I put the bundles in my bag, and I was going to bring them to Dorothy."

"Who's Dorothy?"

"She's the bank employee who has the safe deposit box keys." She dropped the money in her lap as Dorothy's words flashed across her mind. "Mike?"

"What is it? Do you think Dorothy put it there?"

"No, but she made a comment that didn't make sense to me at the time. She mentioned something about how she remembered my box number because she'd just opened it earlier this morning. I thought she was confused, since I'd been in yesterday, not this morning."

He picked up on her thought. "Unless she opened your box for someone else this morning."

"She can't do that, can she?"

"If that someone has a key, she can. Anyone can get into a safe deposit box with the right key and the box number."

Her nervous fingers creased the corner of a thousand-dollar bill, one of many. "Why would someone put all this cash in my safe deposit box?"

"Why would the FBI be questioning you about a man you contacted five years ago?"

"Do you think they're linked?" She sucked in her bottom lip to stop it from trembling.

"If you hadn't had the same suspicion, you never would've run out of that bank."

"As soon as I found the money, I knew something was off—not just that the bank had made a mistake, but that the money represented something sinister. When I walked out into the bank and saw those two talking to Dorothy, I panicked."

"That's understandable." Mike checked the rearview mirror for the hundredth time. "They didn't show up to help you count your money."

Shoveling the bundles back into her purse, she said, "They came to arrest me, didn't they?"

"I don't want to scare you, Claire," he said as he brushed the back of his hand against her arm, "but I think so."

Her mouth felt dry even though Mike wasn't telling her anything she hadn't suspected already. Maybe she'd suspected it from the moment Agents Finnegan and Glotz showed up at her house this morning, flashing pictures of Hamid.

She bolted forward in her seat. "Mike."

"Don't worry, Claire. We'll figure this out."

"It's not that. What about Hamid?"

"What about him?"

"If they're setting me up, they're setting up Hamid, too."

"He's their fall guy."

"But he didn't do anything. Hamid is a good kid, a university student. He tried to help me."

"He must live in the States if they're fingering him as the valet. Is he visiting, or does he reside here?"

"H-he lives here...now. Remember, I told the FBI agents that I'd helped him with a student visa." She stuffed her hands beneath her thighs.

"And he's still here? How long has he been here?"

"Mike, I sponsored him. I facilitated his relocation to the US from Pakistan. He's a student at MIT."

"I heard you tell the FBI agents that you'd helped him, but not that much." Mike groaned and pressed the heel of his hand against his forehead. "That's not gonna look good."

"Let's face it. Nothing's going to look good at

this point. They managed to turn even something as harmless as a safe deposit box into poison for me."

"Correll must know you have something on him—something other than suspicions about your mother's accident, unless he's using the car bomb as an excuse to get rid of your petty meddling and direct the suspicion away from him." He snapped his fingers. "He kills two birds with one stone."

"I really don't care what his motivation is at this point. The question is, what are we going to do now?"

He pointed to the road ahead. "Disappear and regroup."

"Where are we going?"

"Vermont."

"That's so far. What's in Vermont?"

"A safe house, seclusion." He patted the dashboard. "We're going to have to get rid of this sweet ride first."

"Get rid of, as in *get rid of*?"

"I'm not going to send it to a dismantler, if that's what you're thinking. We'll leave it at the airport in Newark and take a very long bus ride to Vermont."

"I want to get to Ethan."

He squeezed her hand. "I know you do, but he's safe where he is, and if you try to see him, they could be waiting for you."

"How did this get so crazy so fast?" She massaged her temples with her fingertips. "Once Prospero identifies the man meeting with Spencer as the same one who executed my husband, will this all end?"

"It's not as simple as that, Claire. We'd have to get more on Correll than just the meeting."

"And I'm supposed to hang out in Vermont—without my son—until you do?"

"It's a start." He tugged on a lock of her hair. "Trust me, Claire. Can you do that?"

"I don't think I have a choice, Mike. You're all I've got."

And she could do a lot worse than Mike Becker.

THE SWITCH AT the Newark airport went smoothly. He parked Claire's Lexus in the long-term parking, buried it among rows and rows of cars so it wouldn't be lonely.

It had been a stroke of luck that he'd taken his laptop and another bag from his hotel room before going to the bank. The FBI probably would've staked out his hotel, and he never would've gotten to his computer.

If that man and woman at the bank were even FBI. He didn't want to worry Claire with his suspicions—yet.

He had cash and documents in his bag and more waiting for him at the cabin in Vermont.

And Claire wasn't hurting for cash. Guaranteed those bills in her safe deposit box weren't marked and traceable. Whoever put them there hadn't expected Claire to make a run for it with cash in hand.

That was one thing he'd learned about his pretend fiancée in the past few days—expect the unexpected. Her stepfather hadn't been paying attention all those years.

The bus slowed to a crawl as it rumbled over the railroad tracks, and Claire turned from the window, her beautiful face pinched with worry.

He knew her furrowed brow and pursed lips owed more to her concern about Ethan and Hamid than for herself. She could worry about them, and he'd worry about her. Someone had to.

"Are you doing okay? We can get something to eat at the next stop. We're not going to be in Vermont until almost ten o'clock tonight."

"Food is the last thing on my mind." She nudged her toe against the bag between his feet. "Are you going to contact Prospero when we get settled in the safe house?"

"Uh-huh."

"Can you bring up the news on your phone and see if we've made the Most Wanted list yet?"

He pulled his phone from his pocket and dropped it into her cupped hand. "Knock yourself out."

He extended his legs into the aisle between the seats and slumped down, crossing his arms over his chest and closing his eyes.

If Prospero found no link between the men in the two videos, he'd have a problem on his hands. He didn't believe for one minute that Claire had anything to do with the assassination of the CIA director, who'd been the deputy director when Shane Chadwick had been murdered, but evidence pointed to her involvement, and others might not see it the same way he did.

Claire nudged his shoulder, and he opened one eye. "I was planning on getting some shut-eye until we hit Philly."

She held up the phone in front of his one eye and said, "Look. They have Hamid's picture out there as a suspect in the car bombing."

He opened his other eye and studied the earnest face of a young man captured in a black-and-white photo. "Did the FBI pick him up?"

"No." She skimmed the tip of her finger along his phone's display. "They can't locate him."

"Didn't you tell me he was at MIT? Does he stay in Boston during the winter break?"

"I have no idea. I wasn't lying to the agents. I haven't been in touch with Hamid for a while."

"Did the article mention your name?"

"No." She held out his cell to him. "Not yet, anyway."

He dropped the phone into his pocket and closed his eyes. "Maybe we'll be in Vermont by the time your name is out there. It's going to be a long night. Let's try to get some rest."

What must've been a few hours later, the low rumble of the bus startled him awake, and his eyes flew open. Claire's head rested against his shoulder, her blond hair cascading down the length of his arm.

He inhaled her scent, which held a hint of dusky rose petals. Her proximity gave him crazy ideas, and he couldn't tell if these ideas were based in reality or had bubbled up as a result of his overriding need to protect a woman in jeopardy, any woman in jeopardy, just like he'd tried to protect his mom all those years.

"Claire?"

"Mmm?" She shifted her head and then jerked it up. "Sorry."

"That's okay." More than okay. "The rhythm of a bus ride always puts me to sleep, too. Looks like we're stopping outside Philly, and I'm starving." He hoisted his bag from the floor to his lap. "Do you want a sandwich or whatever they have at the station?"

"I'll take a sandwich and a diet soda. I'd offer to stay on the bus and watch your bag, but I have to use the restroom."

"I've got it." He hitched the strap of his bag over his shoulder and stood up, swaying slightly as the bus came to a halt.

Mike ducked to look out the window past Claire, and his gut rolled as he took in the multitude of people crisscrossing in front of the station.

Anybody could be out there, but the FBI hadn't gone public with Claire's picture yet. Maybe they were hoping to shield a sitting senator's step-daughter, not that the sitting senator would mind at all.

He knew a little about the perks enjoyed by politicians and their families. Jase Bennett, one of his Prospero team members, was the son of Senator Carl Bennett and used to talk about the privileges his family enjoyed.

He followed Claire down the steps of the bus and took her arm. "I'll get some food, you hit the restroom and we'll meet back on the bus. Fifteen minutes—don't be late."

He watched her head toward the ladies' room, and then he turned the corner in the direction of the food concession. He shuffled along in line, and when he got to the counter, he ordered two sandwiches and grabbed a bottle of water, Claire's soda and a bag of chips.

He stashed the food in his bag and lingered in the hallway outside the restrooms. He hadn't noticed Claire going back out to the bus, but then he hadn't been paying attention. His eye twitched, and he rubbed it. No way had anyone followed them to the airport or followed the bus. He'd double-checked and triple-checked.

Claire must've gotten back on the bus.

He strode outside where the bus spewed exhaust as it idled. He hopped on, and his step faltered. Their seats were still empty.

He scanned the rest of the bus and the passengers that didn't even fill half the seats.

He cranked his head toward the driver. "Do we still have a few minutes? My wife isn't back yet."

"Yeah, I'll wait for you, but not too long." The driver tapped a clock above the windshield. "We're on a schedule."

"Understood." Mike hopped off the bus, his heart slamming against his chest.

He entered the station again, swiveling his head from left to right. He jogged toward the restrooms, his bag banging against his hip.

This time he didn't wait, he shoved open the door to the ladies' room. A woman looked up, her brows colliding over her nose.

"This is the women's restroom."

He bent forward, looking under the doors of all the empty stalls. No Claire.

"Doesn't anyone have any boundaries anymore?"

"I'm sorry. I'm looking for someone."

"That's what the other guy said."

Chapter Eight

Claire stared at the barrel of the gun. She never should've left the ladies' room with him. He wouldn't have shot her with that woman in the other stall.

Would he shoot her now?

She swallowed as she glanced down the alley with the car parked at the end. He just might.

"Just keep walking, Claire, all the way to the end of the alley. It's going to be okay. We don't really believe you had anything to do with the assassination of the director. We want to talk, to protect you."

Her gaze shifted from the gun to the man aiming it, dressed in faded jeans and a dark jacket zipped over a hoodie. Had the FBI changed its dress code recently?

She shook her head. "I'm not going with you. You're going to have to shoot me here."

A slight movement behind the man caught her attention. Mike's face appeared in the opening of the door leading to the bus station. She quickly directed her focus back to her assailant's face.

"Nobody wants to shoot you, Claire. Just get in the car at the end of the alley, and we'll discuss this whole misunderstanding."

"There's no misunderstanding on my part. Someone, my stepfather, is setting up me and Hamid Kahn for the car bombing. Who are you? You're not FBI."

Mike had pushed open the door without a sound, but something must've alerted the man.

He spun around, but Mike had anticipated the move. He dropped into a crouch and then flew at the man, his long leg extended in front of him.

"Get down, Claire!"

She dropped to the cold ground just as Mike's foot hit the man midchest. They both fell over with Mike on top.

The gun skittered to the side of the struggling men and with one fluid movement, Mike grabbed it and drove the butt against the side of the man's head with a sickening thud.

Claire sprang to her feet. "Let's go!"

Mike had his hands buried in the man's pockets. "The money, Claire. Leave the money."

Her movements shifted to autopilot and she dumped the bundles of cash on the ground next to the inert form of her attacker.

Mike grabbed her arm and they barreled back

through the door and ran toward the front of the bus station.

The bus had just closed its doors and Mike banged on the glass. The driver opened the doors. "I almost left you."

Mike panted out his thanks and they stumbled down the aisle to their row.

Claire dropped to her seat, pressing her hands to her still-thundering heart. "H-how did that happen? How did he find us?"

"The money. There must've been a tracking device in the money. I was stupid not to check it."

"He wasn't FBI, no way."

"The FBI didn't bug the cash, either. They still think that money belongs to you, that it's Hamid's payoff. That must be why someone put it in your safe deposit box."

"That guy in the alley? He was Spencer's guy." She brushed some dirt from the knees of her pants. "Are you sure that's how he tracked us down, the money?"

"It must be. I made sure we weren't followed, Claire. Now that you dumped the cash, we should be safe." He put his arm around her shoulders. "Are you okay?"

"I'm fine, shaken up, but fine." She threaded her fingers through his and brought his hand to her cheek. "Are you okay? I thought for sure he was going to shoot you when he spun around."

"I had the element of surprise, thanks to you. Good job not giving away my presence."

"I saw you searching his pockets. Did you find anything?"

"I found a phone, which I didn't take in case it could be tracked, and a couple of other items, which I'll take a look at later—no ID, no wallet, nothing like that."

"Do you think whoever sent him gave him orders to kidnap me or kill me?" Her muscles tensed. Either way, if she hadn't had Mike by her side, she'd be dead meat by now.

He disentangled his fingers from hers and squeezed the back of her neck. "I'm not sure, but this is looking better and better for your story about Correll. The fact that someone other than the FBI was tailing you proves that this is some kind of setup."

"No call to your boss yet?"

"I'll wait until we get to our destination. By now, he's probably heard that you took off. He'll have plenty of questions."

She sighed. "Unfortunately, we don't have many answers for him. If the ID of the man in the two videos comes through, will Prospero have enough information to go after Spencer, along with what just happened in the alley back there?"

"It might be enough to start looking at Senator Spencer Correll more closely." He reached down for his bag and unzipped it. "In the meantime, let's eat."

She peeled back the plastic wrap on the sandwich he'd handed her and spread a paper napkin on her lap. She took a bite and raised her eyes to the ceiling of the bus. "I never thought cold turkey on white bread would taste so good."

"Sorry, that was the only kind of bread available." He unwrapped his own sandwich and took a huge bite.

"I'm being serious. It tastes great."

He popped open a bag of potato chips and shook the bag in front of her. "Want one?"

"No, thanks, but do you have my soda in there?"

"Be careful." He pulled it from his bag. "It's been through the ringer."

She twisted the cap and the bottle hissed at her, so she settled for another bite of her sandwich while the bubbles fizzed out. "I can't wait until this is all behind me. I've been living with it for so long—my husband's death, my mother's death, my suspicions, walking on eggshells around Spencer. I just want a normal life, a safe space to raise my son."

"You'll get there, Claire, if I have anything to say about it." He crunched another chip and she laughed.

"Somehow you don't inspire a lot of confidence with potato chips all over your face." She reached out to touch a crumb on his bottom lip at the same time his tongue darted from his mouth to catch it. When his tongue touched her fingertip, their eyes met for a split second, and she jerked her hand back as if scorched.

"Sorry." The fire continued in her belly and she made a fuss of opening her tamed soda. "I should keep my hands to myself. You're not a five-year-old."

"No, I just had food on my face like a five-year-old." He sucked the salt from the tips of his fingers, which did nothing to quell the warmth that was infusing her entire body.

He balled up the chip bag and cracked open his bottle of water. "You don't happen to have any hand sanitizer in that huge bag you call a purse, do you?"

"Would I be the mom of a five-year-old if I didn't?" She pawed through her bag, happy for the diversion. "Got it."

He held out a cupped palm. "Hit me."

She squeezed the clear gel into his palm and he rubbed his hands together.

"Tell me about Ethan."

"Really?" She dropped the sanitizer into her purse. "You're just trying to get my mind off of things, aren't you?"

"Partly, and partly I want to hear about Ethan. Maybe I'm trying to get *my* mind off of things. I had switched gears into retirement mode, and now I'm on the run to another safe house in a long line of safe houses."

She huddled into her coat. "I'm sorry. You're so good at your job, I forgot this was a second-thought, last-minute assignment for you before retirement. Now you're in it."

He shrugged. "I've learned not to take any job for Prospero lightly, but I do want to hear about Ethan."

"You don't have to twist my arm to talk about my son."

As the bus rumbled north into the night, she slid low in her seat and spoke softly about Ethan. And Mike was right, just as he was right about so many other things—the day's fears and anxieties receded, replaced by warm memories of her son.

Several hours later, as they reached the end of the line, she jabbed Mike in the arm. This time she'd woken up first, which gave her the chance to raise her head from his shoulder. She was pretty sure she'd tipped her head toward the window as she began to doze off, but Mike just had that kind of shoulder—the kind a girl could lean on.

She owed Lola Coburn big-time for sending him her way.

Mike was alert in an instant. "We're here?"

"Yes." She twisted her head around. "And we're among the last few passengers. What next?"

"We pick up our next mode of transportation and then get a good night's sleep."

"We just slept."

He rubbed the back of his neck. "I said a *good* night's sleep, and we still have some work ahead of us before we reach that point."

Mike hadn't been kidding. Once they got off the bus, they picked up what looked like an abandoned car at a junkyard. The keys had been stashed on top of the visor, and Mike had retrieved a black bag from the trunk.

The car didn't have chains, but the snow tires had enough traction to get them safely to a cabin tucked in the woods at the end of a harrowing journey on a two-lane road, just beyond a small town.

Mike pulled the car around to the back of the dark cabin.

"I'm hoping this place has heat and light." She dragged her purse, much lighter without the cash, into her lap.

"It has everything we need for at least a month's stay. Our support team is top-notch."

"A month?" She grabbed her coat from the backseat of the junker. "I hope we're not going to be holed up here for a month."

"It's like the end of the earth up here, isn't it?" He opened the door a crack and the cold air seeped into the car. "Ready?"

"Ready as I'll ever be." She swung her legs out of the car, her high-heeled boots, ridiculously unsuited for a cabin in the middle of the Vermont woods, in the snow.

She slogged through the white stuff in Mike's wake as he trod a path to the back door of the cabin.

He jingled the key chain that he'd picked up from the car. "Our key to paradise."

Tipping her head back to take in the log cabin, she twisted her lips. "You've got a funny notion of paradise, Becker."

"Let's put it this way." He inserted the key in the dead bolt at the same time he punched a code in the keypad she hadn't noticed before. "We have food, water, heat and a bed. Sounds like heaven to me."

He must've heard the breath hiss from her lips because he jerked his head around.

"I mean two beds, of course—clean sheets and everything."

Shoving open the door, he stomped his boots on the porch mat and then reached for a switch on the wall. "Welcome to paradise."

Yellow light flooded the small room decked out like a snug getaway—a trio of love seats hugged an oval braided rug in front of a stone fireplace. End tables carved from logs stood sentry on either side of the love seat facing the fireplace, and a huge set of antlers graced the space above the mantel.

She swept her arm across the room. "Nice

setup…except those antlers. I can't help thinking about the poor buck who lost them."

"Not my thing, either, but I didn't decorate the place." He dropped his bags by the door, closed it and reset the alarm. "Are you hungry? Tired? There's a kitchen, and I'm almost positive there are toiletries in the hall closet—stuff like tooth-brushes and combs. Probably none of the high-end stuff you use."

"Hey, beggars can't be choosers, but I'm not all that tired."

"Hungry?"

She eyed the kitchen on the other side of the room. "What's in there, astronaut food?"

"I'm sure we're low on the fresh fruits and veg-etables and the free-range chicken."

She shrugged the strap of her purse from her shoulder and placed it on one of the log tables. "I'll check it out. You want something?"

"I'm starving."

"When aren't you starving?" She moved into the kitchen and started throwing open the cup-board doors.

"I'm six-four. That's a lot of space to fill. Check the freezer."

She opened the freezer door and the stack of colorful boxes almost made her dizzy. "What do you want? We have lasagna, French-bread pizza, chicken wings, taquitos and a bunch of other stuff. This truly would be heaven for Ethan."

"Make an executive decision."

She peeked around the freezer door at Mike setting up his laptop.

"Are you going to call Jack now?" She grabbed two French-bread pizzas from the middle of the stack and steadied the leaning tower of frozen goodies with her other hand.

"That's exactly what I'm going to do."

"Are you sure there's internet and cell reception out here?"

"Unless the weather has interfered, we'll have reception. We make sure of that before we set up shop in any area. Even going as far as installing our own tower."

"I'm sure the neighbors are thrilled to have you." She placed the two pizzas in the microwave and set the time.

"If we had neighbors. That bus stop was in the nearest town."

While she'd been in the kitchen, Mike had cranked on the furnace and started a fire for good measure.

She sauntered out from the kitchen and sat on the arm of the love seat where he'd set up his computer.

He tapped in a number on his phone, followed by a series of other taps.

"It's Mike." He tapped his display once more. "Jack, I just put you on speaker, and Claire's in the room with me."

Jack's low voice reached out from the phone. "Claire, are you okay?"

"I'm fine. D-do you know what's going on?"

"I know that the FBI suspects Hamid Khan of placing the car bomb that killed the director of the CIA."

"No way, Jack. Hamid is innocent, according to Claire."

"The Fibbies are citing communications between Claire and Hamid, but they haven't named Claire as a suspect yet." He cleared his throat. "And then there's the small matter of the escape from the two agents sent to pick up Claire at the bank."

"Is that what the FBI is reporting?"

"I haven't seen anything official about that from the FBI."

"I'm still working that one out. In the meantime, some guy pulled a gun on Claire at a bus station outside Philly. That means the money in Claire's box had a tracking device hidden in it. You know the FBI doesn't work like that."

Jack whistled. "This has gone beyond informing on Claire to the FBI."

Claire leaned forward. "I knew it was a setup, Jack, and my stepfather's fingerprints are all over it."

"We're working on that, Claire. Where are you, Mike?"

Claire poked Mike in the arm and drew her

finger across her throat. Jack Coburn might be married to one of her oldest friends, but he still worked for the US government, the same government that just might be trying to set her up.

Mike scowled at her. "We're at a safe house, Jack. I'm assuming we can't come in yet."

"No. It's one thing for you to be on the run with Claire, since everyone still thinks you're the hapless fiancé, the cover, but we can't let the intelligence community believe we have any part in this. We can't offer Claire any official protection."

Claire couldn't wait any longer, so she ducked her head and whispered in Mike's ear, "Ask him about the videos."

"Any news on those videos I sent you?"

"Nothing yet, although the evidence is compelling."

Claire sighed, her shoulders sagging. "Finally."

"I thought so, too." Mike squeezed her knee. "No ID yet on the man with Senator Correll?"

"Not yet. If the guy spent most of his career as a terrorist covered up, we might have a hard time linking him to any cells or groups."

"But his eye. That means something."

"Means a lot, Mike. Like I said before—compelling."

Mike picked up the phone as if by speaking into it directly, he had a better chance of convincing Jack. "If we can tie Spencer Correll to terrorist activity, the Agency and the FBI are going to have to look into him for this hit on the director. He's going to step into Haywood's shoes any day now."

"He'll need confirmation first, and that's not gonna happen before the holidays. The deputy director will run things for now."

"We need to make that connection, Jack. Isn't there still a heightened alert at the White House for Christmas Day?"

Claire sucked in a breath. This was the first she'd heard of that.

"There is, or there was until McCabe discovered all of Tempest's plans."

Claire folded her arms and tapped her fingers against her biceps. They'd just lost her. She didn't know a McCabe and had no ideas what a Tempest was, except that she was in one.

"The assassination of Haywood could be part and parcel of the same attack." Mike rubbed his knuckles across the scruff on his chin.

"We considered Tempest as soon as we heard about the car bomb. All I can tell you is we're on it, Mike. We have your back."

"And Claire's?" Mike shifted his gaze to her and watched her beneath half-mast lids.

"As long as you're with Claire, we have her back, too."

"I'm with Claire, Jack. I'm staying with her. That's why you sent me on this assignment."

"That's before she became a suspect in a terrorist attack."

"I'm still on the phone, Jack." She clenched her jaw.

"I know, Claire. I'm sorry, but we have relationships to maintain. We gave you Mike, and that's all we can do right now."

Her tight lips curved into a smile and she dropped her hand to Mike's back. "And I thank you for that."

The two men ended the call and Mike collapsed against the back of the love seat. "Life would be so much easier right now if they could ID the man who murdered your husband and link him to the man meeting with Correll."

"I've been saying that for five years." The sadness tugged at the corner of her lower lip.

Mike dabbed the rough tip of his finger on her cheek. "I'm going to make this right for you, Claire."

The gesture and the sentiment made her lip turn up again. "You don't have to fix anything, Mike. The fact that you're here, on my side, means everything."

She covered her mouth and jumped from the arm of the love seat. "The buzzer for our French-bread pizza went off a while ago. I hope they're not ruined."

He called after her as she scooted into the kitchen. "They're French-bread pizzas in the microwave. What could possibly be ruined?"

She punched the button that released the door

on the microwave and the cheesy smell of the pizzas wafted out. She removed their cardboard cooking containers and slid each one onto its own plate. "Water?"

"Are there bottles in the fridge?"

"Yeah, no beer, though." She tucked the water bottles under her arm and carried the plates out to the living room. "Since the FBI hasn't outed me as a suspect yet, is it okay if I use your phone to check in on Ethan?"

He handed her his cell. "Sure, but don't give anything away."

She placed the call and chatted briefly with Ethan's grandmother since Ethan was already sleeping. Nancy Chadwick assured her that Ethan and Lori had arrived safely and mentioned that they'd be out snowboarding all day tomorrow.

Claire ended the call, followed by a long exhaled breath. "Here's your phone, thanks."

"Everything okay in Colorado? Nobody sounded suspicious?" He looked up from digging in his bag, his hands full.

"Everything's fine. I put your water on the table."

"Yeah, I could use a beer. The safe houses don't contain any alcohol, but there's nothing stopping us from picking up a six-pack in town tomorrow."

"Yeah, nothing but that *America's Most Wanted* poster with my face plastered on it that could go up any day now." She settled on a cushion at right angles to Mike, her knee bumping one of his long legs.

She pointed to the items in his hands as he put them on the love seat next to him. "What's all that?"

"The stuff from your phony FBI agent's pockets." He picked up his pizza and crunched into it.

"He's not *my* phony FBI agent." She placed a paper towel on his thigh. "High-class all the way."

Mike devoured his pizza with a few more bites and wiped his hands and mouth. "No ID, but let's see what this guy deemed important enough to carry with him on an abduction."

She shivered and picked a triangle of pepperoni off her pizza.

Mike held up a red-and-white hard pack of cigarettes. "Smokes, a key, some change, a little cash—not as much as he has now."

"Maybe he should take the money and run. I can't imagine Spencer or his cronies being very forgiving of his failure."

Mike held up a card, running his finger over the embossed lettering on the front. "Interesting. A plumber's business card. I think I'm going to have some questions about my pipes."

He had placed each item on the table at the corner of their two love seats, and Claire picked up the key. "I wonder if this is the key to my safe deposit box. He could've been the one to deposit the money."

"The bank has to have cameras on that room. You'd think the FBI would've looked at that tape by now to determine if you really did deposit that money."

"The fact that they probably did and it didn't prove my innocence is slightly troubling." She toyed with the cigarette carton. "This feels empty."

Mike shrugged and chugged some water from his bottle. "Open it."

She flicked the lid open with her thumb and peeked inside the box at the crumpled silver packaging. "It is empty."

Mike's dark brows formed a V over his nose. "Why would he carry an empty cigarette box in his pocket?"

"There's this." She plucked the foil wrapping, which had been rolled into a ball, from the box and bounced it in her palm.

"He's gotta have something in there. Drugs?"

She pinched the edges of the wrapper with her fingers and pulled it apart. "Maybe drugs or medication."

"What's in there?"

She held out her hand to Mike, where five little blue pills lolled in the foil.

Mike's features sharpened and two spots of color formed high on his cheekbones.

"Mike, what's wrong?" She could barely form the words in her suddenly dry mouth.

He closed his hand over hers and the blue pills.

"If Correll really is behind this action against you, then he's involved with a terrorist organization—the worst—and the danger to the White House is back on the table."

Chapter Nine

Claire's eyes widened and something in their violet depths flickered. Did she understand that bad news for the country meant good news for her?

Of course she did. There wasn't much Claire Chadwick didn't understand except maybe that her obsession with getting justice for her husband and then her mother had put her life on hold and, even worse, in danger.

He could detect the movement of her Adam's apple in her slender throat as she swallowed. "These blue pills mean something to you?"

He squeezed her hand before releasing it and them. "You heard me mention Tempest on the phone just now, didn't you?"

"Yes." She crumpled the foil in her fist and stuffed it back into the cigarette box with the tips of her fingers. "It didn't mean anything to me then and it doesn't mean anything to me now."

"It's a covert ops organization, like Prospero, deep undercover. In the past few months we've become aware that they've been using their power to destabilize the world."

"What have they been doing?" She trapped her hands between her knees and hunched forward.

"Assassinations."

"Just like Director Haywood." Tilting her head to one side, she gathered her hair in her hand and twisted it into a knot. "What do the blue pills mean?"

"Tempest has agents, just like we do. But unlike Prospero, Tempest has been experimenting with its agents—drugging them, brainwashing them."

She ran a thumb between her eyebrows. "That man at the bus station in Philly was one of these agents?"

"Looks like it." He flicked the cigarette box with his long fingers. "I'll send these in for analysis, but the coincidence is too great."

"So, since Spencer sent this man after me, this superagent, that proves he's in league with Tempest, doesn't it?"

"*If* your stepfather is behind the death of the director and ordered that man to abduct you."

"We're back to that."

"We have no proof Spencer Correll is involved in anything—including your mother's accident."

"Unless we get a match on those videos."

"And this latest discovery just might light a fire under that investigation." Mike grabbed his phone again and called Jack, pressing the speaker button.

"Nothing's changed, Mike."

"It has here, and you're still on speaker."

"What's up?" Jack's voice lost its bored edge, and Mike nodded to Claire.

"I emptied the pockets of the man who tried to abduct Claire from the Philly bus station, and I just made a crucial discovery." He reached for the cigarette pack as if he needed concrete verification. "He had some blue pills on him, and they look exactly like the T-101 pills Max Duvall showed us."

Jack whistled through the phone. "If Tempest is in DC and was responsible for the director's murder, they might still be plotting something bigger for the White House, just like McCabe said."

"And Correll just might be the guy on the inside of it all."

"If we can tie him to Tempest and this setup of Claire."

"The videos, Jack." Mike tossed the cigarette pack back on the table. "ID the guy in the videos."

"We're on it. In the meantime, send us those pills for analysis."

Mike ended the call and cupped the phone between his hands. "If there's anything else you can think of, Claire, now's the time."

"Maybe Hamid knows something."

"You can't just give him a call on his cell phone. If he's off the grid, he probably dumped his phone already."

She slumped back in the love seat and stretched her long legs in front of her, tapping her boots together. "I've been thinking about that."

"Don't look at me." He threw up his hands. "Believe it or not, Prospero doesn't have a line on every suspected terrorist in the US."

"Hamid is not a suspected terrorist." Her eyes glittered at him like jewels through the slits of her eyes.

"He is now." He tapped the display of his phone, where she'd read the news about Hamid on the bus.

"In the beginning of our association, Hamid and I communicated via a blog, more like an online discussion group."

"The FBI already tracked your communication with Hamid. That's why they dropped in on you in DC."

She shook her head and her blond locks caught the low light from the lamp on the table next to her, giving a glow to her face, already animated with this new idea. "Once Hamid got to London, we stopped that form of communication. There was no more need for it. He was no terrorist and I was helping him gain entry to the US on a student visa. The kid is seriously a genius."

"Your communications with him from that point on were out in the open?"

"For all the world, and the FBI, to see. There's

no way the Feds know about our back-and-forth on this website prior to Hamid's arrival in London."

"How can you be so sure?"

"Because I communicated with others in this discussion group, as well. They picked out, or my stepfather led them to, Hamid because he's the only one they knew about. That's the stuff they traced."

He rubbed his chin. Prospero would want to talk to Hamid, anyway. Claire could do the work for them to bring him in. "So, you'd try to make contact with Hamid through this blog? How do you know he'll check it?"

"I don't, but there's a good chance." She drew her knees up to her chest and wrapped her arms around her legs. "If Hamid is in trouble, he's going to try to reach me. He knows I'll try to reach him, too. He knows I have connections, political connections. What he doesn't know at this point is that it's those connections that got us both into trouble."

"Give it a try." He twisted to the side, grabbing his laptop. He logged in, entered a few passwords and launched a web browser. Holding the computer in front of him, he rose from his seat and positioned the laptop on Claire's thighs. "Do you remember the URL?"

"Absolutely." She tapped his keyboard while he circled around behind her on the love seat.

He hunched over the back, peering over her

shoulder as the page filled the window, populated with pop-up ads for clothing and instruments and music lessons. "What kind of discussion group is this?"

"On the surface?" She clicked several links on the page in rapid succession. "It's a blog and discussion for people looking for musical hookups, but in reality it's a message board for people who want to hide their communications."

"Really?" He squinted at a variety of messages on the page. "Whatever happened to using the drafts folder of a shared email account?"

"I haven't heard about that method. Have you ever had to use it?"

She jerked her head around so suddenly, her nose almost collided with his chin. He reared back. "Sorry. Didn't mean to get into your personal space. My damned eyes are getting worse and worse since I hit forty."

She snorted. "Yeah, you're a pathetic physical specimen."

Her gaze swept across his shoulders and down his arms, still wedged against the back of the love seat. His nearness gave her butterflies in her belly—just like a high school crush. He could get into her personal space as much as he wanted.

She patted the cushion next to hers. "Sit here. You can see better, even though all I'm going to do is post a message. Right now I don't see anything that could be from him."

Her side of the cushion sank when he sat next to her, causing her shoulder to bump against his. She left it there.

"Would he use his real name?" He ran one finger down the list of posts on the screen.

"He's Einstein—for obvious reasons."

"And you're…?"

She wrinkled her nose as her cheeks warmed. "Paris."

"How'd you come up with that?"

"Hamid actually came up with it himself." She shrugged. "He's a fan of American pop culture, and I'm the only blond heiress he knows."

"Makes perfect sense to me. What are you posting?"

Her fingers hovered over the laptop. "I just want to let him know we can help."

She chewed her lip and started typing.

Mike read her words aloud as she entered them. "'Everything okay with the band? I think we're in the same boat. Let me know if you need a backup singer.'"

She clicked the button to post her message under the username Paris. "If he sees that, he'll know what I mean."

"Why so cryptic if the message board is a safe zone?" He took the computer from her lap and logged off.

"You can never be too careful." She raised

her arms, stretching them toward the ceiling and yawning.

"It's past midnight. You gotta be tired even after all that so-called sleep on the bus."

She jerked her thumb over her shoulder. "I haven't even looked past the bathroom in here. Are there two bedrooms?"

"Yes. Do you want to check them out first and call dibs?"

She wanted to call dibs on him.

She stuffed the thought back down into her tired brain. She wanted Mike Becker because he believed in her and it had been a long time since anyone had believed in her. It couldn't be real attraction. She didn't have time for that.

He crouched before the fire to douse it, and her gaze traveled from his broad shoulders, down the length of his strong back and settled on his tight backside encased in worn denim.

He believed in her *and* he was as hot as that fire he was smothering. The sensations pummeling her brain and body emanated from overwrought emotions and pure lust—nothing more.

She forced her languorous muscles to move and pushed off the love seat. "Do you know if the beds are made?"

"Should be."

She clicked on the hall light and poked her head into the first bedroom—standard-issue bed, including sheets and a turned-down bedspread, a dresser, and a small nightstand sporting a lamp and a clock radio.

She crossed the hall to the other bedroom, where a king-size bed dominated the room and a dark chest of drawers stood in the corner.

"You can have this room."

He appeared behind her, and she jumped.

"You okay?" He placed his hands on her shoulders from behind and the warm breath caressing her ear made her heart beat a little faster.

"On edge."

"I can't imagine why." He pinched her shoulders. "I found some toiletries in the closet and left them for you in the bathroom—toothbrush, toothpaste, soap. What were you just saying?"

"You can have this room." She flung out her arm into the space. "You need the bigger bed."

"Are you sure?"

"Besides, the other room has a mirror. I'm going to need to spend long hours in front of that mirror tomorrow morning to fix myself up after the day I had today."

"You did have a rough day, and yet—" he shifted to her side and cupped her face with one hand "—you still look beautiful."

A pulse thrummed in her throat and she parted her lips to protest, to assure him she hadn't been fishing for a compliment. She never got the chance.

He swept his lips across hers, and when she

didn't make a move, not even a blink of an eyelash, he pressed a hard kiss against her mouth that felt like a stamp. He pulled away just as abruptly.

"Get some sleep, Claire."

"G-good night." She sidled past him out the door and practically flung herself into the bathroom across the hall.

She slammed the door behind her and hunched over the small vanity, almost touching her nose to the mirror. She couldn't.

She hadn't been with a man since she lost Shane. Her attraction to Mike felt like such a betrayal to her dead husband.

A sob welled up from her chest and she cranked on the water in the sink, letting her tears drip down her chin and swirl down the drain with the water.

She'd kept telling herself that she'd let go once she found justice for Shane, but maybe she'd been fooling herself. Once Shane's killer was brought down, would she have another excuse?

Maybe Mike Becker had been sent not to save her from Spencer, but to save her from herself.

THE NEXT MORNING she shuffled into the living room in the same jeans and sweater from yesterday and wedged her hands on her hips as she watched Mike make coffee in the kitchen. "No fair."

He looked up, a lock of dark hair falling in his

eyes. "What's not fair? I said you could have the bigger bed. Do you regret your generosity now?"

"I'm not talking about that." She perched on one of the stools at the kitchen island that doubled as a table. "You're wearing different clothes."

"From the bag I took from the hotel." He pinched the gray material of the waffle-knit, long-sleeved shirt away from his chest. "Luckily I had some casual clothes in there."

She folded up the sleeves of her blue cashmere. "This used to be one of my favorite sweaters, but I'm pretty sure I'm going to be sick of it by the end of the week."

"We can get you some clothes—not those designer duds you favor, but there are a few stores in town."

"Do you think I need to wear a disguise?" She fluffed her hair. "I can color my hair, but I refuse to cut it."

He cocked his head to the side. "You'd look good as a redhead, but those eyes..."

She blinked. "What about them?"

"They're violet."

"Only sometimes, and so what?"

"I can't imagine anyone looking into those eyes once and being able to forget them."

"You're waxing very poetic this morning." She jumped from the stool and pulled open the freezer door, inhaling the iciness from its depths in the hopes it could cool down her heated blood. "Anything for breakfast in here?"

He clinked some cups behind her. "I'm not exactly sure what 'waxing poetic' means, but I'm sure I've never done that before in my life. Coffee?"

"Do you like playing the poor, rough boy from the streets?" She yanked a box of breakfast sandwiches from the inside door. "Does that usually work for you with the ladies?"

She clutched the cold box to her chest, afraid to turn around. But Mike laughed, and she spun around to face him.

His lopsided grin had her warming up again despite the frozen breakfast pressed against her body.

"The poor, rough boy from the streets *does* work with the ladies, but I never once thought you'd be susceptible to the act. Are you?"

She smacked the box on the counter. "Nope."

"Hey, watch that. You're breaking my…breakfast."

"No news from any quarter yet?" She needed to get this conversation and relationship back on the business track. They didn't have to play engaged couple anymore.

"I don't know about your discussion board, but I haven't heard anything from Prospero." The coffee dripped to a stop and he poured two cups. "The news media are still flashing Hamid's picture, but you haven't even been mentioned as a person of interest yet."

She raised her eyes to meet his. "That's not good, is it? I mean, if a legitimate agency like the FBI is after me, at least I know they're not going to shoot me on sight."

"But we don't want your picture and name splashed all over the media, either."

"At least the Chadwicks have no idea what's going on. Should I call them again to find out if they've heard anything?"

"Don't invite trouble. If you act suspiciously, you're putting them on the spot if the FBI goes out there to talk to them."

Her hand trembled slightly as she picked up her coffee cup. "I don't want that. They've been through enough."

"Ethan's safe with them and Lori." He wrapped his hands around his own cup. "Lori's reliable?"

"She's wonderful. Ethan adores her." She narrowed her eyes. "Why do you ask?"

"At breakfast yesterday morning I caught the tail end of something between her and Correll."

"Ugh, yes. He's propositioned her a time or two, but she came right to me." She blew on the surface of her coffee, wishing for some half-and-half. "Lori can handle herself. She's tougher than she looks. She's actually a former army nurse."

"Impressive." Folding his arms, he leaned against the kitchen counter. "Correll had a thing going on with his admin assistant, too, right? Fiona? That's how you got into his laptop in his office."

"That's right." She tapped her head. "The eyes may be going, but you're not senile yet."

"Thank God."

"Why did you bring that up?"

"Would Fiona be willing to do more snooping for you? For a price, I mean."

"She might be, although I think she's still sleeping with him."

"After he cheated on her?" He reached for his cup and took a sip of coffee. "Some women don't know when to quit."

Was he talking about Lori, her or his mother?

She turned away and slid her thumb beneath the seam of the box. "A little jewelry can go a long way. Do you want me to contact her?"

"We'll keep her in our toolbox."

"We have a toolbox?" She pulled two plastic-wrapped frozen sandwiches from the box and held one up. "Looks like egg and sausage on an English muffin."

"Sounds good to me."

She ripped open the plastic with her teeth and placed the sandwiches on a plate. "Is this town safe for us?"

"The FBI hasn't released any info about you yet. I'm positive we weren't followed, once we got rid of that money." He tugged on the end of her hair. "And you need some fresh clothes."

"I just might risk getting nabbed by the FBI for a change of clothes at this point."

"We'll be fine, and I need to go to the post office and send off these pills."

With visions of new clothes before her eyes, Claire wolfed down her breakfast almost as quickly as Mike did.

As she rinsed their cups in the sink, she asked, "Can you log in to your laptop so I can check the message board?"

"Sure." He wiped the crumbs from the counter and swept their trash into a paper bag.

"Ah, a self-sufficient bachelor."

He was beside her in an instant with a dish towel. "I've had years and years of practice. Now hand me that mug so I can dry it and put it away."

He put the dishes in the cupboard and leaned over the counter where his laptop was charging. He powered it on and entered his thousands of passwords before spinning the computer toward her. "Go for it. I'm going to brush my teeth before we head into town."

With a little hitch in her breath she accessed the discussion board and scanned the messages. She blew out a breath. Nothing much new and nothing from Hamid. Her message waited for an answer.

"Anything?" Mike came up behind her smelling like mint.

"Not yet, but I'm confident he'll check this board."

"If you say so." He logged off and slipped the computer into the bag. "I'm taking it with me, so we can check again while we're out. Let's get ready to go."

"I'm going to brush my teeth and pull my hair back."

When she returned to the living room, she joined Mike, standing in front of the mirror by the front door.

He pulled a fur-lined cap with earflaps low on his forehead. "How's this? Do I fit in?"

She turned the flaps down over his ears, brushing his hair back. "You look like any other Northeasterner in the winter."

"I'd still be more comfortable with a bit of a disguise." She wound a dark scarf around her neck, covering the lower half of her face. "What do you think?"

"It's a start." He threw open the closet door next to them and pawed through the coats. He yanked one off its hanger and held it up. "You'd look less like you with this cover-up than with that long, black coat that screams well-heeled city girl."

She glanced at her coat draped over one of the love seats and stepped forward to take the dark green down coat from Mike. But he held it open and said, "Turn around."

She did so, and he draped it on her shoulders, his fingers skimming the sides of her neck. She shivered as she stuffed her arms into the sleeves. Why did his touch always feel like an electric current dancing across her skin?

The down coat fell right above her knees, leaving a gap of denim between the hem and the top of her black boot.

She finished the look by twisting her ponytail into a knot on top of her head and pulling a red cap over it. She arranged the scarf around her neck and face.

"Nobody's going to recognize me out and about, but as soon as I take all this stuff off there goes my disguise."

"Like I said, after what happened in Philly, I don't think Correll is anxious for the authorities to pick you up. I think he'd rather use his own methods."

Despite Mike's implication and the frisson of fear tingling down her spine, her lips stretched into a smug smile. "You did it again. You mentioned my stepfather, so you do believe he's behind this."

"I always believed you, Claire. We just need to prove it."

"We'll prove it, and Hamid is going to help me."

"If he ever gets that message."

"He'll get it." She pointed to her boots. "I suppose there are no snow boots here, are there? Walking in the snow in these heels is hell, and walking on ice is going to be even worse."

"There might be some boots in the mudroom in the back. What size?"

"Eight."

He disappeared down the hallway and came back with a pair of snow boots. "These are a men's nine. Do you think you can manage until you buy something in town?"

"Walking in boots that are too big for me can't be any worse than four-inch heels." She changed shoes and then followed Mike into the winter wonderland. She huffed out a breath and watched it freeze in the air. "If there's snow in DC, I guess this is what you get in Vermont."

Mike started the engine of the car and cranked on the heat and defrosters. Then they both got to work on the front and back windshields, clearing the ice from the glass.

They hopped into the car and made the slow, winding drive back to the small town of Maplewood.

Her knees bounced as they drew closer to civilization. Had the FBI plastered her picture all over the place like Hamid's, or did Spencer have his own private hell planned for her that didn't involve the authorities?

What would the good people of Maplewood do

if they recognized her? Make a citizens' arrest? Would the Maplewood PD try to take down a terror suspect?

Her eye twitched. How could anyone believe she'd throw her lot in with terrorists when she'd spent the better part of the past five years in her own private war against them?

Spencer had used her former instability and irrational threats against Deputy Director Haywood to set her up, and she'd walked right into his trap.

But he didn't know she'd have Mike Becker in that trap with her. Did her stepfather still believe her fiancé was a politically naive salesman from Chicago?

Let him. Spencer had unwittingly walked into a trap called Prospero, and he'd pay the price.

"Are you nervous?" His gloved hand ran down her arm, making the slick material of her coat whisper.

"Nobody followed us up here, right?"

"That's right."

"Of course, we thought that before when we dumped the tracker, my phone and then my car, and they still caught up with us."

"My fault." He returned his hand to the steering wheel. "The money was a foreign object introduced into our environment. I should've checked it out before allowing you to bring it into the car."

"As I recall, we were in a hurry when I brought that money into the car. An FBI agent was literally hanging on to my coattails, or what I thought was an FBI agent."

"Then after." He raised his shoulders. "I should've examined it later. Total fail on my part."

"You redeemed yourself by saving me in the alley."

"I'll redeem myself when this is over and you're safe."

"Mike?"

"Yeah?"

Her lip trembled and she clasped her mittened hands together in her lap. "I won't know what to do when it's over. I won't know who I am."

He wheeled the car into a parking space in front of the local post office and cut the engine. "You'll be one tough chick who never gave up and who will be able to face anything—even if that anything is the monthly PTA meeting."

Her nose stung and she sniffed. "I think I can handle a PTA meeting."

As they walked into the post office, Claire kept bundled up in the chilly interior of the building. Her gaze darted among the items on display, half expecting to find her mug on a wanted poster.

Mike selected a priority mail pouch and shoved the cigarette box inside, the blue pills nestled in the box.

He paid the clerk with cash and asked, "Is there a women's clothing store nearby? My wife needs to pick up a few more warm items."

"Down about two blocks there are a couple of stores." She tossed the package into the wheeled cart behind her and gave Mike his change. "It sure is an early winter this year. Maybe it'll be a short one."

"We can only hope." Mike rapped his knuckles on the counter. "Thanks, and happy holidays."

When they got outside, he asked, "Can you walk a few blocks?"

"Absolutely not." She kicked up one foot. "These boots are practically falling off my feet."

They got back in the car and crawled down the street until a few clothing stores came into view.

"Ready to shop till you drop?"

"Sure. I'm not picky."

He dropped his jaw in mock astonishment. "I don't know much about clothes, but I'm pretty sure yours cost an arm and a leg."

"I mean," she said, punching his arm, "I'm not picky when faced with wearing the same thing day after day. I'm really not high maintenance. You should've seen me when I was with the Peace Corps in Guatemala. Not a designer thread in sight."

"You were a Peace Corps volunteer?"

She nodded as she grabbed the car door handle. "It's where I met Shane."

On the sidewalk, Mike stopped in front of a newspaper dispenser. "I need some reading material while you try on clothes."

"I won't be that long, but you can check out the news on me and Hamid, if there is any."

She scurried into the store while Mike fed some coins into the dispenser.

A clerk looked up from folding sweaters. "Good morning. Can I help you find something?"

"Just some casual clothes. I didn't pack enough for this cold."

"I hear you. It's crazy for December, even for us." She plopped a sweater on the pile and turned toward rows of cubbies on the wall. "We have jeans on this side, and even snow pants if you need them."

"I just might need them." Claire fingered the slick material of a pair of black snow pants hanging on a rack.

The little bell above the door rang as Mike pushed his way into the store, the newspaper tucked under his arm.

"Can I help you?"

He waved the paper at Claire. "I'm with her."

"Well, you're in luck. We have a few chairs outside the dressing room just for the gentlemen."

"Perfect." He collapsed in one of the chairs and said, "Knock yourself out, sweetheart."

Claire rolled her eyes and stationed herself in front of the array of jeans, scanning the labels for her size.

After she selected a few pairs of pants, she browsed the long-sleeved T-shirts and sweaters.

With her arms piled high with clothes, she approached the clerk. "I'm ready to try these on."

She flicked Mike's newspaper as she walked by. "Do you want me to model anything, *sweetheart*?"

"You look good in everything, babe."

The clerk smiled as she unlocked the dressing room for Claire. "You have a keeper there."

"Don't I know it?" *He even takes out bad guys with a flying leap and roundhouse kick to the midsection.*

She shimmied in and out of several pairs of jeans, dropping more in the keep pile than not. She pulled on sweaters and shirts and held on to anything halfway decent.

She called out, "Do you want me to leave the clothes I'm not buying in here, or do you want them?"

"I'll take care of them."

Claire loaded up her arms and squeezed out of the dressing room. She brushed past Mike. "That wasn't too bad, was it?"

"No."

The curt response had her twisting her head over her shoulder, and she nearly dropped her clothes in a heap.

The relaxed, loose-limbed man in the chair had been replaced by a tense one, vibrating with alertness, every muscle in his body primed for action.

Her gaze dropped from his face to the newspaper open in his lap. He must've read something about her, something bad.

"Oh, you're taking all those?" The clerk held out her arms for Claire's finds.

"Y-yes. These'll do. I also need some under-wear."

"Long underwear?"

"Yes, and panties, bras."

"In the back."

Mike had folded the paper and joined the clerk at the counter.

Claire rushed to the back of the shop and scooped up several pairs of underwear and a couple of bras in her size—they'd have to do. She couldn't spend one more minute in this store.

The clerk bagged her purchases while Mike pulled out a wad of bills. They clearly hadn't needed the money from the safe deposit box, since Mike carried oodles of what he called untrace-able cash.

He couldn't get rid of it fast enough as he paid for Claire's clothes.

If the friendly clerk had noticed a change in Mike's demeanor, she was too polite to react to it. "You two have a great day, and stay warm."

Mike nodded and Claire said, "You, too."

When they hit the sidewalk, burdened with bags, she spun toward him. "What happened? What did you read in that newspaper?"

"In the car." He popped the trunk and they tossed the bags inside.

When they got inside, Mike dropped the folded-back paper in her lap and jabbed his finger at an article, poking her thigh in the process. "Look at this."

She glanced at the black print in her lap, heaving a sigh. At least her face wasn't plastered there.

She held up the paper to the light coming through the window and read. "'Gathering to honor fallen CIA director. The White House announced plans to pay tribute to Gerald Haywood, the director of the CIA, who was killed in a car bomb on Tuesday in Georgetown, with a gathering of his friends and colleagues, both domestic and international, on Christmas Day.'"

She trailed off. "So? Isn't that to be expected?"

"Don't you get it?" He grabbed the paper from her hand, crumpling it in his fist. "The attack on the White House is back on—and this is the venue."

Chapter Ten

Mike paced the living room of the small cabin. He'd already contacted Jack, and Prospero was formulating a plan to infiltrate the gathering.

Even though Tempest knew Prospero's agent, Liam McCabe, had uncovered its plans for an attack at the White House, it hadn't deterred Tempest. They were going forward with the attack—Mike was sure of it.

When he passed by Claire for the hundredth time, she grabbed his arm. "Sit down and relax, Mike. You're going to wear a hole in the floor."

He raked his fingers through his hair. "I can't believe they're going through with it. They have to know Prospero is going to pull out all the stops to foil them."

"That's good, then. They're so single-mindedly crazy, they're not thinking straight." She squeezed his biceps. "Have one of those beers we picked up."

His eyebrows collided over his nose. "It's lunchtime."

"You know what they say—it's five o'clock somewhere."

He narrowed his dark eyes. "You're calm about this whole thing."

She stepped back from him. "I'm not happy about it, if that's what you're implying."

His eyebrows jumped to his hairline and then he took her in his arms, wrapping her in a warm embrace. "I didn't think that for a minute. Nobody could blame you for feeling satisfied on some level that your gut instincts were right."

"I don't care about that right now." She grabbed handfuls of his shirt and tugged. "I'm going to get you that beer."

"Okay, you win."

He dropped his arms, and a chill flashed across her body. She shouldn't have been so eager to break that clinch. Whenever Mike held her, or even touched her, he gave her a sense of safety and security.

If she was honest with herself, Shane had never given that to her. He'd been all about the thrill first and safety—his and hers—second.

She shook her head to dislodge the disloyal thoughts then went into the kitchen and grabbed two bottles of beer from the fridge.

She rummaged through the utensil drawer until she found a bottle opener. "Do you want yours in a glass?"

Instead of an answer, she heard tapping. She

leaned back to see into the living room. Mike was on his laptop, clicking away. "I thought you were going to relax?"

"We haven't checked your message board in a while…and no glass."

She opened both bottles and returned to the living room, where she stood in front of him, holding out his beer. "It's happy hour."

Glancing up, he said, "I'm all logged in. Whenever you're ready."

Her fingers were itching to attack that keyboard and check for a message from Hamid, but they both needed ten minutes to breathe.

When he'd explained the significance of that White House gathering, she'd been as freaked out as he was, but for once she wanted to be the one with the calm exterior. Mike had been keeping it together for her through it all, and she wanted to prove she could keep it together, too.

She hadn't quite figured out yet whether she wanted to prove she could be calm and collected to Mike or herself, but both had value.

"Skol." She lifted the bottle and then tilted it to her lips and took a swig of the malty brew.

He reached up to take the other bottle from her hand. *"Skol."*

He shoved the laptop from his legs. "Have a seat."

"That's better." She settled on the love seat next to him and touched the neck of her bottle to his with a clink. "Tell me about your last assignment with Prospero."

"This is my last assignment with Prospero."

"I mean your second-to-last. What were you doing before Jack asked you to check in on his wife's crazy friend?"

"It's top secret." He put his finger to his lips, but his frame had stiffened and the lines on his face deepened.

"Are you serious?" She dragged her gaze away from his delicious mouth. "You've already told me plenty of—what I can only guess is—classified information. Hell, you've let me use your secure phone and laptop."

"Because you're involved in this case." He took a sip of his beer. "I'd be breaking a code if I told you about anything else."

She toyed with the opening of her bottle. "That must get lonely."

"Lonely?"

"Keeping everything to yourself all the time."

"There are other things to talk about besides work."

"The weather?" She laced her fingers around the bottle of beer. "You're not exactly forthcoming about your personal life."

He was in midsip and he choked on his beer. "Really? Given the amount of time we've had to talk about anything but our current situation, I think I've revealed a lot."

"You know what?" On an impulse, she reached out and brushed a lock of dark hair from his forehead and then studied his face. "I think you have. You've parsed it out between car bombs, fleeing from the FBI and an attempted kidnapping, but I actually know quite a bit about you."

His eyes widened and his nostrils flared as if he was getting ready to take flight. "Have I been going on and on about my pathetic childhood?"

She laughed and took another chug of her beer. "I'd hardly say you over-shared. It's good. I'm glad I got to take a little peek behind the curtain."

"I'll have to watch that curtain thing, but you know I had it better than some and worse than others. That's the way it goes. At least I had Coach to guide me through a lot of stuff, or I probably would've ended up on the wrong side of the law."

"I'm grateful you didn't, but I apologize."

"For what?"

"This was supposed to be a relaxing interlude between stops in Crazytown, and I had to dredge up stuff you're clearly not comfortable discussing."

"You know what?" He took the bottle from her hand and rose from the cushion. "It wasn't so bad telling you about it."

"Anytime. God knows my life could fill a couple of volumes." She wiped her damp fingers on her new jeans and pulled the computer into her lap. "Time to check on Hamid. Was there anything in that paper about him?"

"Just that they had no leads on his whereabouts."

"That makes all of us." The screen displayed a prompt for a password. "You need to reenter your password. I guess happy hour lasted too long."

He returned from the kitchen, wiping his hands on a dish towel. He bent his long frame over at the waist and entered his password while covering her eyes with one hand.

He was serious about his security.

"While you do that, I'll put together some lunch. I'm glad you insisted on stopping at a grocery store to pick up some fresh food."

"I couldn't handle any more of that frozen stuff." She entered the address for the message board and held her breath as she scanned the page. She squealed.

"He responded?"

"Yes, I got a message from Einstein. He wrote that he is in the same boat and he needs backup." She looked up. "We've got to help him, Mike."

"We can bring him in."

"By bring him in, you mean what? Not take him into custody?"

"Protective custody, not an arrest. Prospero can protect him on an unofficial basis, but we'll want some intel from him." He ducked into the fridge, so she couldn't see his face.

Hopefully, he was telling the truth. "I honestly don't think Hamid has any intel."

"He was set up somehow and he may have noticed something leading up to it, talked to someone, had an encounter. We'll want to know all that."

"So, should I suggest a meeting? He's not going to agree to meet with anyone but me."

"He's not going to have a choice. You're not meeting him alone." He reappeared hugging an armload of veggies. "Is he still online?"

"I don't think so, but I'm sure he'll be monitoring this board."

"Set it up."

"I don't even know where he is."

"Find out, Claire."

She drummed her fingers on the computer. "He's not going to want to meet in Boston, too close for comfort."

"DC's out."

"Would we be safe in New York? We could drive down in about five hours, park and take a subway into the city."

"Crowds aren't necessarily a bad thing. It should be a public place for everyone's safety."

"A club with noise and music."

"Sounds like a plan." Mike waved his knife in the air. "Do it."

She followed the rules of their cryptic communication, suggesting they meet at a jazz club in Chelsea, a place she'd told him about before.

She posted the message. "That's it. Now we wait. If he can't get to Manhattan, we'll move to plan B."

"It's always good to have multiple plans." He began chopping on a cutting board.

She carried the laptop with her to the kitchen counter and set it down. "Do you want some help?"

"When the water boils, dump in the pasta." He jumped back as the oil sizzled in the pan on the stove top. "Where are we meeting him?"

"We? I still think I should meet him alone. He might not agree to see me if I'm with someone, and if I don't tell him, he might bolt when he sees you."

"Like I said before, he doesn't have a choice." He shoved the contents of his cutting board into the olive oil in the pan and stirred, the aromatic scent of garlic filling the kitchen. "You just happened to know of a club in Manhattan where we could meet?"

She dumped the fettuccine into the roiling water and added a pinch of salt. "The kid likes jazz, of all things. He was visiting the city on a break and asked me for a few recommendations. He went to the 629 Club in Chelsea, so I thought he'd feel comfortable in a place he'd been to before."

"You like jazz?" He tapped the pot of boiling pasta with his knife. "Stir that so it doesn't clump."

"Who are you, Emeril Lagasse?" But she dutifully dipped the long plastic fork into the bubbling pot. "Yeah, I like jazz. You?"

"Jazz? Most of it sounds like weird, disjointed noises to me."

She rolled her eyes to the ceiling as she stirred. "Let's see…tough guy from the streets…my guess is rock and roll."

"Easy guess."

"I like that, too. I like all kinds of music." She held up the fork with a few strands of pasta dangling from it. "What do you think? Al dente?"

"Hasn't been long enough." He pinched the steaming pasta between his fingers anyway and dropped it into his mouth. "Too chewy. You can rip up that lettuce and dump the rest of these vegetables in there, though."

She made the salad while he hovered over the stove. "I suppose longtime bachelors learn how to cook, learn how to use the microwave or go out to eat a lot."

"My mom taught me how to cook a few things, but I definitely know my way around a microwave and I have every take-out menu from every restaurant within a five-mile radius of my apartment."

"Your apartment." She plunged a pair of tongs into the salad. "My God, I don't even know where you live. Where do you hang your hat when you're not gallivanting around the world or pretending to be someone's fiancé?"

"Chicago." He bumped her hip with his in the small space of the kitchen to get to the pasta.

"But that's where you grew up, right?"

"Is that a surprise? Wouldn't you have stayed in Florida where you grew up if your mother hadn't married Correll?" He grabbed the handles of the pot and lifted the boiling pasta from the stove. "Watch out."

She scooted over and he dumped the water into a colander in the sink. "Yeah, but my childhood wasn't…" She put two fingers to her lips.

"A nightmare?" He shrugged. "The one person who made it a nightmare is in prison…again, so Chicago isn't so bad. I'm not sure about retiring there, but I'll go back once this is over."

Once this is over. Maybe once this was over, she'd return to Florida with Ethan. Maybe Mike would want to flee to a warm climate to escape the Chicago winters once in a while.

Reaching around him, she opened the fridge and took out the Italian salad dressing they'd bought earlier.

Mike put the finishing touches on the pasta, adding a couple of sprigs of fresh basil, and they sat side by side at the counter to eat their lunch.

"Mmm." She twirled her fork in the fettuccine. "This smells good and it looks almost too pretty to eat."

"Maybe I'll open a restaurant when I retire."

She stabbed a tomato. "You're too young to retire completely. Would you want to work as a security contractor?"

"I'm done, Claire."

"You thought you were done when you took this job, didn't you? You figured you'd be reassuring some woman with an overactive imagination and then you'd be going home to Chicago."

"That about sums it up, but now that I'm here, now that I'm in this with you, I'm in it all the way."

They finished their meal and both reached for the plates at the same time. "I'll do this. Check the message board."

She poured herself a glass of water and sat back down on the stool, pulling the laptop toward her. "It went to sleep. I need you to log in again."

He leaned over and punched several keys. "It's all yours."

She sucked in a breath when she saw a response from Einstein. "It's here. He's good with it. He's already in Queens and he remembers where the 629 Club is. Ten o'clock okay?"

"That'll give us plenty of time to drive down and then catch a subway into the city. He knows enough to watch for a tail, doesn't he?"

Raising one eyebrow, she said, "His uncle is Tamar Aziz. He's been watching his back his whole life."

Mike turned from the sink, the dish towel wrapped around his hands. "And you know for sure Hamid has nothing to do with his uncle's activities."

"I'm positive. I told you, Hamid is the one who told me to look closely at the right eye of the man who murdered Shane."

"Wait. You never told me that before. How'd he know about the coloboma?"

"He wouldn't say directly, but I'm pretty sure he got that particular bit of information from his uncle."

"All right, then." He smacked the towel against the counter. "Looks like we have a date to listen to some jazz."

MIKE DIDN'T LIKE IT—not at all.

Their journey south through the snowy landscape couldn't have gone any better. The white flakes coating the fields and decorating the trees had plunged them into their own personal and interactive Christmas card. With the heat blasting and music playing on an oldies station, Mike felt like he was exactly where he should be in retirement.

Except he wasn't retired. He had one more job to do, and because this job had gotten personal, it was proving to be more stressful than all the assignments he'd had over the life of his career.

Even more stressful than the previous one that he'd bungled.

Coming into the city, dressed in its holiday finest, had made it worse. The closer they got to the club, the more resentment he'd felt toward the Christmas shoppers with their normal lives and their normal families.

He used to feel that resentment because that normalcy was something he feared he'd never have. Now the resentment burned even brighter because he felt as if he were closer to it than he'd ever been in his life.

He'd found a woman, in Claire, who gave him hope that he could have a family without the expectations of perfection. He couldn't do perfection, but he knew he'd never hurt Claire the way his father had hurt his mother.

The dissonant sounds of a saxophone in distress assaulted his ears, and he peered into the bowels of the dark club. "That sounds like an elephant in distress…or in love. I haven't decided yet."

Claire jabbed him in the ribs. "Have a little respect."

"Do you see him yet?"

A pretty African-American girl with a hippie vibe approached them, the beads braided in her hair clicking. "Are you looking for a seat? There are a couple of tables near the bar."

Mike shouted over the noise from the stage, "We're meeting someone."

Claire tugged on his sleeve. "I see him. Thanks."

The hostess bowed her head and slipped through the black curtain that separated the front door from the interior of the club.

"This way." Claire grabbed his hand and led him through the small tables where all the patrons sat facing the stage.

As they neared a table in the corner by a hallway, a young man half stood up, the whites of his wide eyes glowing in the darkness.

"Claire?" Hamid's gaze darted toward Mike's face.

"He's helping us." She pulled out her own chair and hunched over the table toward Hamid. "This is Mike. Mike, Hamid."

Mike shook Hamid's hand, damp with sweat or the beads of moisture from the drink he was nursing.

"You look good, Hamid. How's school?"

"Are you serious?" Hamid glanced to his left and then his right, looking exactly like a fugitive on the run. "It was fine until a friend told me the FBI was looking for me."

A waitress, balancing a tray of drinks on her hand, dipped next to the table. "What can I get you?"

The club had a two-drink minimum, but Mike had already discussed the importance of sobriety with Claire. His gaze dropped to Hamid's glass, empty except for a few half-melted ice cubes. Obviously, the kid hadn't gotten the memo.

"We'll have a couple of beers, whatever you have on draft."

She slapped down two cocktail napkins and melted back into the gloom.

Mike rapped his knuckles on the table in front of Hamid. "Someone gave you a heads-up about the FBI?"

"A couple of friends in Boston. I was already on my way to visit another friend in Queens."

"Why'd you immediately take off, think the worst?" Mike folded over a corner of the napkin.

"I'm at MIT, not living under a rock. When that car bomb went off and killed the director of the CIA and then two FBI agents came looking for me, it gave me a bad feeling."

"Had anyone been following you?"

"Following me?" He swallowed. "Why would they follow me? Wouldn't they just arrest me?"

"Not sure." Mike smoothed out the napkin. "Not if they wanted to see if you were meeting with anyone."

The waitress returned and put two beers on the table, along with another cocktail for Hamid.

He folded both hands around the short glass and took a long drink.

When he put the glass down, Claire reached over and squeezed his hand. "Take it easy, Hamid.

We're going to help you. Mike's...agency can bring you in."

"Oh, no." Hamid held up his hands. "I'm not going with anyone, not the CIA."

"Mike's not CIA, and you can't be out here on your own." She grabbed Mike's hand so that she was forming a human chain with the two of them. "I'm not."

With his other hand, Hamid snatched up his cocktail napkin and wiped his forehead. "When I saw that message from you, I really got spooked, Claire." He licked his lips. "What's going on?"

"We're being set up. That's all I can tell you."

Mike broke Claire's grip on his hand. Kumbaya time was over. He asked him in Punjabi, "What can you tell us, Hamid?"

Hamid's eye twitched, and he spoke to him in English. "Are you CIA? Claire, is he CIA?"

Claire glared at him, her eyes pools of liquid violets. "He's not. Why would I be with a CIA agent when I'm under suspicion myself?"

Hamid licked his lips. "Are you? Are you really? Because I haven't seen your name and picture in the papers like mine."

"Tell us what you know, Hamid. Did anyone contact you before the bombing? Did you hear anything from your uncle? Why did you tell Claire to zero in on that assassin's eye? What do you know about him?"

A bead of sweat rolled down Hamid's face and

he rubbed his glassy eyes. Either the kid couldn't handle his booze or he was coming down with something.

"That man," he said, then coughed and continued, "they called that man the Oxford Don."

Claire gasped. "Why didn't you tell me that before, Hamid? You told me nobody knew who he was."

Hamid took another gulp of his drink. "C-couldn't tell you. They used him for propaganda, for high-profile executions."

"Where is he?" Claire had curled her fingers around the edge of the table. "Where is he now?"

Hamid choked and a trace of saliva trickled from the corner of his mouth.

Mike started from his seat. "Do you need some water?"

Claire leaned in close to Hamid and whispered, "Where is he?"

Hamid pitched forward on the table and murmured something Mike couldn't hear above the din coming from the stage, and then his hand jerked and his breath rattled.

"Hamid." Claire nudged him and then turned to Mike. "Is he okay?"

Mike reached over and felt the young man's pulse. "He's dead."

Chapter Eleven

Claire shook Hamid's lifeless arm. "Hamid, wake up."

Every fiber in Mike's body quivered on high alert as his gaze darted around the dim, crowded club. She obviously hadn't processed what he'd just said. "He's not asleep, Claire. He's dead."

"What?" The face she turned to him was drained of all color, and the perfect oval stood out in stark relief against the murky backdrop. "How?"

"Poison would be my first guess."

"What?" She patted Hamid's black hair. "Who?"

"Claire, we need to get out of here—right now."

Her head jerked up and her hair fell over one eye. "Here? Someone here killed him?"

"Shh." He shifted his body in front of Hamid's slack form as he glanced toward the hallway leading to the bathrooms. "I'm hoping there's an exit that way."

"W-we can't leave him here."

"Do you suggest we carry him out? Call 9-1-1?" He took a breath and trailed his fingers down her arm. "I'm sorry, Claire. We have to leave him here, and we have to leave now."

As if on cue, the drummer launched into a solo. Mike stood up and slipped his hand beneath Claire's arm. "Let's go."

She followed his order as if sleepwalking, throwing one backward glance at Hamid's inert form.

Mike led her toward the hallway in the back of the club with his heart pounding. His step quickened when he spied the green exit sign above a metal door.

Nobody had followed them down the hallway, but Claire's body was now trembling more and more with each step. He whispered in her ear, "It's okay. We're almost there."

When they reached the door, he pushed on the horizontal release bar. He held his breath, waiting for the alarm. If there was one, he couldn't hear it above the drummer.

The cold air blasted his face, and he ducked his head against it, pulling Claire close to his body. She matched him stride for stride down the alley, although he could tell she was on autopilot.

They burst out onto the street and merged into the foot traffic, still heavy at almost eleven o'clock at night. People rushing home with their packages, filled with Christmas spirit, leaving no dead bodies behind in clubs. A curbside Santa rang his bell and they both jumped. Mike took a deep breath.

"You're doing great, Claire. Just keep on moving." He steered her toward the subway entrance and down the stairs, cranking his head over his shoulder.

He hadn't noticed anyone following them, either from the bar or picking them up on the street, but there must've been someone in the bar. Someone had spiked Hamid's drink. Maybe their own beers had been drugged. Someone had either followed Hamid to that location or they'd picked up on his communication with Claire.

Grabbing Claire's hand, he kept her close as he jogged down the stairs. He fed money into the machine to buy two single-ride tickets, the blood pounding in his ears, lending urgency to his actions.

A man rounded the corner behind them, clutching something beneath his long black coat. Mike curled his hand around his own weapon in his pocket while yanking Claire in his wake. "We need to hurry, Claire."

He nudged her through the turnstile and the clattering sound seemed to rouse her from her petrified state.

Her stride lengthened until it turned into a jog, and they ran together toward the train squealing to a stop. The doors flew open and they jumped on as one.

Mike continued moving, dragging Claire along with him, making a beeline for the next car as he kept one eye on the other passengers boarding. The man with the coat was not among them.

The train swayed into motion, and Claire grabbed on to the bar above her. She swung into a seat and closed her eyes.

Mike took the seat next to her, still assessing the other passengers.

He finally let out the breath trapped in his lungs and took Claire's cold, stiff hand in both of his. She must've left her gloves in her pocket. He rubbed some warmth back into her flesh.

"I'm sorry, Claire."

Her eyes clicked open like a doll's and shifted sideways to his face. "We got him killed."

"We don't know that." He tucked a strand of hair behind her ear. "They'd made Hamid. They knew just where to find him."

She shook her head, dislodging the lock of hair again. "They couldn't have known about that message board. No way."

"If they tapped into his computer, they'd know his every keystroke, or maybe they put a tracker on his phone. I have a hunch they didn't realize he'd be meeting you."

"Why do you say that?" She finally turned her head and met his eyes.

"I could be wrong, but my guess is that his first drink was already drugged. They wouldn't want him dead before we even got there."

"Maybe our drinks were drugged, too. I didn't even have a sip of mine, did you?"

"No, thank God." He slipped an arm around her. "I just can't believe they'd let us get away that easily if they'd still been there."

"They drugged all our drinks and left."

"There's no way of knowing at this point."

A tear rolled down her cheek and she made no move to catch it, so he brushed it away with the pad of his thumb.

"Don't blame yourself, Claire. It's the fault of those who dragged him into this, set him up and then murdered him. I'm not sure he would've come with us, anyway. He was too spooked."

"H-he betrayed me. He'd been lying to me all this time."

"You mean about the man who executed Shane?"

"He knew. He knew who he was all along, or he at least knew more than he was telling." She pressed her fingertips against her temples. "I was so naive. Hamid was using me, probably to get into the US."

"Don't be so hard on yourself, Claire, or on Hamid." He caressed her shoulder. "You two helped each other at the time. Maybe he protected you by keeping you away from the truth. He understands that world better than you do."

"Did you hear what he said? He called him the Oxford Don."

"We knew he was English from his accent. That's not a surprise, and I've never heard that name before, so it must've been just among the locals."

"But at the end. He whispered something to me before he...died."

His pulse quickened. "He actually whispered something that you understood?"

"I leaned forward to catch what happened to be his last words."

"I didn't realize he'd said anything to you. What was it?" The corner of his eye twitched and he rubbed it.

"I'd asked him about the Oxford Don. I asked him where he was now."

"Did he answer you?" The air between them stilled.

"It doesn't matter." She lifted her shoulder. "He said something that made no sense at all."

"What did he say?"

"Caliban. He said the Oxford Don was with Caliban."

CLAIRE JERKED BACK from the expression on Mike's face. His jaw hardened and his dark eyes

glittered with an emotion she couldn't fathom…
but it scared her.

"What? What is it?"

The train lurched into the next station, and her
gaze bounced from the sign outside to the map of
the line inside the car to make sure they weren't
missing their stop.

Mike's body had tensed up beside her, and she
bumped her shoulder against his. "Mike? Does
Caliban mean something to you?"

"Claire, I can't believe this." He dragged his
long fingers through his hair until it stood on end.
"This is all linked somehow—Shane's execution,
the car bombing the other night, Tempest."

"Wait." Icy fear gripped the back of her neck.
"What are you talking about? How is Shane's
death linked to Tempest? What is Caliban?"

The train screeched to a stop, and Mike took
her arm. "Let's get back to the cabin. Are you up
for driving all night?"

"Maybe it'll take that long drive for you to explain everything to me."

They linked arms, huddling together against
the cold night and the dark forces that seemed to
be closing in on them.

When they got back in the car, their first stop
was a drive-through coffee place, where Mike ordered a large black coffee and she got a decaf hot
tea.

She had a feeling that Mike's story would be

enough to keep her awake on the long drive back to their cabin in Vermont. She also had a feeling that after hearing the story, she'd want to stay in that cabin forever, keeping both Mike and Ethan close to her side.

When they got back on the road, Mike slurped at his hot coffee and turned down the radio. "Caliban is the head of that agency I told you about—Tempest."

She drew in a quick breath. "And the man who killed Shane is now connected to Caliban, to Tempest?"

"It would seem so if that's the name Hamid gave you, and it doesn't mean that Tempest was responsible for Shane's kidnapping and murder. Caliban could've recruited this Oxford Don later. Tempest wasn't active five years ago."

"Who is this Caliban? Does anyone know? Does Jack know?"

"We think he's former US military."

"Spencer knows him."

Mike jerked his head toward her. "How do you know that for sure?"

"I'm just guessing, but it makes sense. He probably knew him before Caliban became the evil mastermind behind Tempest."

"There has to be some way to tie Correll to Tempest and stop this attack against the White House."

Claire stretched her cold hands out to the vent

on the dashboard blasting warm air. "And to clear me, right? I mean, that's still a priority for you, or is it all about stopping the attack on the White House?"

His hands tightened on the steering wheel and his knuckles turned as white as the snow outside the car window. "Of course it is. That's still my number one objective."

Or it was until he found out he was poised to foil one of the most significant terrorist attacks in the world. She didn't want to delve too deeply into Mike's priorities right now.

Reaching for his cell phone in the cup holder, she asked, "Is it okay if I check your phone for some news?"

"I don't think you're going to find anything about Hamid in the breaking news right now— too soon—but hold up the phone and I'll punch in my code."

She complied and said, "I'm just wondering if I'm in the news yet. If I'm not, you know Tempest plans to take me out just like Hamid."

He finished his code and she swept her finger across the display to wake up the phone.

"Claire, we can't even link Correll to Tempest or Tempest to Hamid."

"But all the puzzle pieces are there, aren't they?"

She tapped the screen and scrolled through various news sources as Mike drove on through the night and the falling snow. On the way in to the city, even though they'd been coming in to meet Hamid, the mood in the car had been almost festive. The music, the conversation, the scenery had all contributed to a sense of normalcy, but all that had changed with Hamid's death and his dying words.

The name of Caliban had dropped between them like a curtain. It had propelled Mike back into his covert world, where he kept secrets from her.

She stumbled upon an article about the White House gathering to honor the director and as she skimmed it, she let out a snort.

"This is interesting."

"What's that?" Mike smacked his cheek and took another gulp of coffee.

"Are you okay to drive? Do you want to switch?"

"A Florida girl driving in the snow? I can handle it." He jerked a thumb at the phone. "What's interesting?"

"I'm reading a short news brief about the ceremony honoring the director. It's more of a name-dropping puff piece, but it looks like Spencer is taking Julie Patrick."

"Who's Julie Patrick? The name sounds familiar."

"She's English, the widow of Benedict Patrick,

and a major shareholder in Brit-Saud Oil. She's a big political donor and philanthropist."

"Sounds about right to me. If she's a mover and shaker in political circles, it doesn't surprise me that Correll knows her."

"Oh, he not only knows her—" she dropped the phone back in the cup holder "—he dated her. It looks like my stepfather is zeroing in on another rich widow."

Mike snapped his fingers. "The secretary."

"Huh?" She yawned and rubbed her eyes. "What secretary?"

"Correll's secretary—Fiona, the one who got you into his computer before, allowing you to copy that trashed video, the video that started it all."

She blinked. Maybe she should've gotten some coffee. "What about her?"

"Claire." He tapped his temple. "She gave you that info before when she'd believed Correll had moved on. If that's the case again, maybe you can use that to tap into more information. Would she help you again if she felt Correll had used her and was moving on to greener and richer pastures?"

She scooted forward in her seat, her fingertips tingling with excitement. "She might. Fiona is all about Fiona."

"If you contacted her, would she tell anyone?"

"Not if we sweetened the pot with some money.

If she can make money on the deal *and* stick it to Spencer, she'll be all in."

"We can do that, offer her money."

"I'll contact her tomorrow and see what she can do for us." She slumped down in the seat, bunching the coat into a pillow and stuffing it between her shoulder and the window. "I'm going to make myself comfortable for the rest of the trip. Let me know if you need a break from driving."

"Relax, Claire. I'm good."

She drifted in and out to the monotone of talk radio and Mike's hushed call to Jack, the slick material of the coat whispering under her cheek every time she shifted position.

She wanted to be Mike's priority. She wanted to be someone's priority for a change. She squeezed her eyes shut against the self-pity. She usually didn't indulge...must have been the exhaustion.

Just as she found a good spot, Mike brushed her cheek with his knuckle. "We're almost at the cabin. Did you sleep?"

"In fits and starts. You must be exhausted."

"I had my thoughts to keep my mind busy— and the caffeine to keep me awake."

He pulled around to the back of the cabin, and Claire pressed her palm against the car window. "We just left here this afternoon, and I feel like it was a lifetime ago."

"Hamid's lifetime."

The cloud layer had cleared and the sun was

poised to make its full ascent. The snow sprinkled on the tree tops sparkled under the early morning rays.

She crunched up the pathway to the back door behind Mike. What now? It was too early to contact anyone. Mike had already called Jack to fill him in on Hamid and Hamid's last words, and the gulf had widened between her and Mike.

All she wanted to do right now was curl up and get warm, on the inside as well as the outside.

Mike ushered her inside the cabin and turned up the furnace. "Let's warm this place up."

"Exactly what I was thinking."

"Are you hungry?"

"I can't even..." She covered her eyes with one hand. "No."

"What happened to Hamid—not your fault, Claire."

"I—I..." Was that what he thought, that she still blamed herself? That had been her immediate response when Hamid collapsed on the table in front of her, but she'd long ago given up feeling guilt for the horror that seemed to dog her steps.

But the concern in Mike's eyes? Addictive.

"I just can't help feeling that if we'd never contacted him, he'd be alive right now."

"I don't think so." Mike took her by the shoulders. "They had him pegged for the fall guy long before you posted that message on the board. I don't think they even knew he was meeting us last night."

"That makes sense, but it still hurts." She drove a fist against her chest. "It hurts here."

And she meant every word. Hamid had been her protégé. In a way, he'd been her lifeline after Shane lost his life in the most brutal way. Even now that she knew Hamid had been holding out on her, she mourned his death.

Mike's grip on her shoulders softened. "You have dark circles under your eyes. You need some sleep."

She needed him, but her seduction skills were rusty, and dark circles beneath her eyes wouldn't cut it.

"I'd like to take a warm bath first. I'm just so chilled." Again, no lie.

"Good idea." He pointed at the kitchen. "Do you want me to make you some hot tea while you run the bathwater?"

"That would be perfect."

They brushed past each other, her on her way to the bathroom and he on his way to the kitchen.

Once inside the claustrophobic bathroom, she spun the faucets on the tub. Unfortunately, the keepers of the safe houses hadn't thought to stock bubble bath or scented candles.

She shed her clothing and almost felt as if she was casting off the past five years of her life, a celibate life paying homage to the memory of a dead husband, a husband who'd never put her first.

The steam from the tub curled up in welcome invitation. She cracked open the bathroom door and then stepped into the bathtub, sinking into its warm embrace.

Stretching her legs out, she braced her toes against the porcelain at the end of the tub, bending her knees slightly. She shimmied her shoulders beneath the lapping water and cupped handfuls of it, splashing her thighs.

The tap on the door set the butterfly wings to fluttering in her belly. It had been a long time since she'd seduced a man.

"I'm in the tub."

"Are you warming up? I have your tea."

"I feel like I'm melting." She turned off the water by gripping the faucets with her toes. "You can come in with the tea."

He pushed open the door and froze as his gaze collided with hers. "Sorry. I thought you'd have the shower curtain drawn."

"It was a little too claustrophobic for me."

"Okay." Keeping his gaze trained at the ceiling, Mike shuffled into the bathroom, holding the cup of tea in front of him. "Just warn me if I'm going to trip over the toilet or something."

"You're good, just a few more steps. It's not like the bathroom is cavernous." She sat up in the tub, the water sluicing off her body, and held out both hands to accept the tea.

The toe of Mike's bare foot hit the side of the tub and he went into a crouch, extending the cup. "Got it?"

She curled her fingers around the cup, brushing the tips along Mike's knuckles. "Thanks. Can I ask you two more favors?"

"Sure." He backed up, still averting his gaze from the tub.

"Can you bring me that T-shirt of yours I wore to bed last night, and can you get a fire going?"

"Absolutely." He smacked the doorjamb on his way out and called back, "That T-shirt looks a lot better on you than me, anyway."

Claire placed the cup on the edge of the tub and slid down until the water lapped at her chin. She blew out a breath, creating a flotilla of bubbles.

She'd set the stage even though Mike had been too much of a gentleman to take a peek at her bare breasts. She cast her eyes downward. Yep, she still had 'em.

Mike tapped on the door again. "Here's the T-shirt. I'll hang it on the doorknob inside and work on that fire."

The white T-shirt swung on the handle as Mike snapped the door shut. Claire's mouth twisted into a frown. Seemed as if *she* needed to work on that fire.

She flicked up the stopper with her big toe and

yanked the towel from the rack. She shivered as she patted herself dry. It was time to warm up— for real.

She pulled Mike's T-shirt over her head and released her hair from its knot, the tendrils at her neck damp. Fluffing her mane, she leaned in close to the mirror and touched up the drugstore makeup on her face leftover from yesterday.

A full-on makeup job would look a little ridiculous, but she was no twentysomething who could get by on good bone structure alone, especially after the night they'd just had.

Tugging on the hem of the T-shirt, she made her grand entrance.

Mike looked up from his phone, and something flickered in his dark eyes, something almost predatory. Her long catlike stride faltered as those butterflies took up flight again in her stomach.

She was supposed to be the aggressor here, so she pinned back her shoulders and continued her saunter toward the love seat facing the fireplace. When she reached it, she fingered the edge of a blue blanket.

"I thought since you were wearing a T-shirt, you could use the extra warmth."

"Thanks, but this fire feels great." She dropped to the edge of the love seat and held up her hands, palms out, to the flames dancing in the fireplace. Being bundled up in a blanket would hardly add to her sex appeal.

"I can get you closer." He came up behind her on the love seat and pushed it and her a few feet closer to the fireplace.

Reaching around, she squeezed his biceps. "You've got some muscles there, big boy."

"What are you doing, Claire?" He straightened up and folded his arms over his chest.

Her cheeks blazed as hot as the fire. She'd been such an idiot. Just because the man had never been married, it didn't mean he didn't have experience with women and wouldn't catch on to what she was trying to do. With his looks and manner, he probably had women across the globe trying to seduce him on a regular basis—women a lot more adept than she.

"I thought…" She bit her bottom lip to stop the lie. Tears puddled in her eyes at her pathetic behavior. "I just didn't want to take a backseat to Tempest, even though I know that's where I belong."

The tight look on Mike's face dissolved and he clambered over the back of the love seat, as if he couldn't wait to be next to her. "What are you talking about? You are my priority right now. You're not in the backseat and you don't deserve to be in the backseat."

She laced her fingers together and dropped her head to study her nails. "The minute I told you about Caliban, you got this look in your eye—a gleam of excitement and anticipation—like you'd finally found a purpose in this whole tangled web."

"Am I really that transparent?" His big hand covered both of hers. "That pathetic?"

"Pathetic? You? I'm the one who plotted a seduction to make you like me again."

"Really? You were seducing me?"

She snorted. "Now, *that's* pathetic. You didn't even realize that was a seduction."

"It never occurred to me that a beautiful widow, obviously hung up on her dead husband, would be seducing me."

"Is that how you see me?" She tilted her head to look into his face. "Hung up on Shane?"

"You've spent the better part of five years skating on the edge of danger trying to identify his assassin. How would you describe it?"

"I want justice for him."

"And justice for your mother."

She jerked back. "Of course."

"What about you?" He rubbed a circle on her back. "What about Claire?"

"I—I don't need justice."

"Maybe not justice, but you need a break from all this. You need to put yourself first, Claire."

"I put Ethan first." Her tense muscles were screaming at her. She didn't want to have this conversation with Mike. He saw too much.

"I know you do." He hand crept up to the base of her neck, where his fingers kneaded her taut muscle. "Outside of your child, you need to start putting yourself first—because nobody else ever has."

The truth, voiced aloud by someone else, punched her in the gut, and she doubled over. "Sh-Shane."

"Shane left you for a story opportunity in a dangerous part of the world, knowing full well the US government does not negotiate with terrorists. He walked into a trap, blinded by visions of a Pulitzer."

"Why are you saying this? You sound just like my stepfather."

"God help me, but Correll was right about that."

She bolted up from the love seat, but Mike was beside her in a second, grabbing her around the waist. "Give yourself a chance, Claire. Give yourself a chance at life…at love."

Her body stiffened as she tried to hold her world together, and then Mike crushed her against his chest. He bent his head to hers and pressed a hard kiss against her lips, which parted under his assault. Then he thrust his tongue inside her mouth.

She wanted to repudiate him, reject everything he'd said about her and Shane—reject the truth. Digging her fingers into his back, she squirmed in his viselike hold.

He broke off the kiss that had seared her lips and then released her, catching her arm as she staggered back. His dark eyes kindled with that predatory look again and he growled deep in his throat. "Say the word, woman. Just tell me no—once."

Her chest heaved with each ragged breath she took, the thin cotton of Mike's T-shirt abrading her erect nipples adding pain to the pleasure that surged between her legs. Never breaking eye contact, she twisted out of his grasp and knocked his arm away.

A pulse throbbed in his throat, and the line at the side of his mouth deepened. Holding up his hands, he took a step back.

She licked her bottom lip, wedging the tip of her tongue in the corner of her mouth. Then she pinched the hem of her T-shirt and pulled it up one inch at a time, watching the fire reignite in his eyes.

She hadn't bothered with underwear after her bath, and when the T-shirt hit her waist, Mike's gaze dropped, scorching her, weakening her knees. She rolled the shirt over her breasts, heavy with desire and aching with need.

Yanking the T-shirt over her head, she tossed it behind her, standing in front of Mike totally naked, bared to his scrutiny and judgment.

He reached out and cupped the back of her head, entangling his fingers in her hair. He took possession of her lips again, walking her backward until the backs of her calves brushed against the cushion of the love seat.

The fire crackled and spit behind him, the glow highlighting the silver in his hair. He tugged gently on her hair, lowering her to the love seat. As she sat down, he hovered above her, her lips still captured by his.

By the time he broke the seal of their kiss, molten lava coursed through her veins, pooling in her belly—and below.

He traced a finger from the indentation of her throat to her mound, and she quaked at his touch. He knelt in front of her and opened her legs by placing his palms on the insides of her thighs.

His dark head moved toward her and she curled her fingers in his thick hair. The touch of his tongue made her gasp and throw her head back.

His lips against her swollen folds teased her to dizzying heights and she had to force herself to take a breath before she passed out.

The minute she took a sip of air, her world shattered. She raised her hips and Mike slipped his hands beneath her bottom and rode out her orgasm with her, his tongue still probing her depths as she shuddered and sighed.

She felt boneless and breathless as Mike hunched forward and cinched his hands around her waist.

He kissed the corner of her mouth and whispered, "That wasn't a no, was it?"

"I don't even remember the question."

He draped the blanket around her shoulders and lifted her in his arms.

"I'm too tall to be carried around."

He hoisted her higher. "I'm taller."

He took her into his bedroom and yanked back the covers on the bed, then placed her on the cool sheet. "You can take a nap in here."

She pulled on his T-shirt. "Is that what they're calling it these days?

"I meant, you can take a nap after I ravish you. Unless…" He pulled off his shirt and dropped it onto the floor.

Sitting up on her knees, she ran her palms across his well-defined chest. "Unless what?"

"Unless you want to kick me out after what I said about Shane."

Her hands stilled. "You were right. I never felt that Shane valued me, or at least he didn't value me as much as he did his career."

She hooked her fingers in his waistband. "I don't want to talk anymore."

She didn't want to put Mike on the spot, didn't want to force him to choose between her and his career. She always lost that battle.

Running her hand up his thigh, she pressed a kiss against his collarbone. "I don't want to talk."

As she unbuttoned his fly, he buried his hands in her hair and kissed her mouth. She slipped her hands inside his boxers and caressed his erection.

"Mmm, I don't think you've forgotten anything." He nuzzled her neck. "Your touch feels so good."

She helped him peel his jeans from his hips, and then she fell back on the bed, beckoning with her hands.

He kicked off his pants and straddled her, his knees on either side of her hips. She took him in her hands again, reveling in the feel of his smooth, hard flesh.

"I want you, Claire. I've wanted you from the minute I saw you on that balcony looking like the snow queen." He eased into her. "Do you believe me?"

Did it matter if she believed him? From the way that he kissed her and the way his body shuddered when she ran her nails along the bare skin of his back, she knew she was his priority—right now. And all she had was right now.

He filled her completely and asked again, "Do you believe me, snow queen?"

Closing her eyes, she whispered, "Yes. Yes, I do."

HER EYES FLUTTERED open and the gray light in the room mimicked the gray fog in her head. She had no idea what time it was or even what day it was. Hell, she could barely remember her name after the thorough lovemaking last night…this morning.

Mike's breath warmed the nape of her neck

and she wriggled against him, feeling his erection come to life against her backside. She could wake up to *that* for the rest of her life.

Mike kissed the curve of her ear. "Did you get enough sleep?"

"I think so." She yawned. "What time is it?"

He'd obviously already looked at his watch or his phone because he answered promptly, "It's four forty-five."

"P.m.?"

"Of course, unless you think we slept for twenty-four hours."

"I really have no concept of time right now." She shifted onto her back. "Do you think there's any news about Hamid?"

She might as well be the one to bring them back to cold, hard reality. She didn't want him to think she actually believed she'd remain his priority in the face of this developing plot.

"Not sure." He reached for his phone, and his eyebrows collided over his nose. "I got about ten texts and voice mails in the past thirty minutes."

"What?" The sensuous languor that had seeped into her body evaporated, and she bolted upright. "Who are the texts from?"

Before Mike could answer, the room exploded around them.

Chapter Twelve

The blast rocked the floor and slammed Mike into the wall. His eyes watered as he blinked against the acrid smoke filling the room.

"Claire!"

"I'm on the floor. What happened?"

"Put your clothes on, but stay close to the floor. I have to get my bags from the other room."

"Wait! There's fire, and my clothes aren't in this room."

"Stay on the floor and cover your face with the sheet. I'll be right back."

"Mike! No!"

Crouching low, he put his T-shirt over his head and charged out of the bedroom. He collected a few of Claire's things from the room across the hall and ventured into the living room to get his bag of money and weapons and his computer.

Hot spots of fire dotted the room and flames engulfed the ceiling above the front door. He clasped his bags to his chest and loped back to the bedroom where he'd left Claire. The room where they'd just spent a morning exploring each other's bodies and an afternoon wrapped around each other in satiated sleep had suffered the least damage—but he knew there was more to come.

He burst into the room and tossed Claire's clothes in her direction. "Get dressed."

"C-can we get out that way? Through the front door?"

"We're not exiting this cabin through the front door."

"What? Is it so bad? The back? Can we get out through the back?"

"Enough questions, Claire. Put your clothes and shoes on. Take whatever you can in those plastic bags."

He hurried into his own clothes and whipped back the carpet on the wood floor. He ran his hands across the planks until he felt an edge.

He slipped his knife from his jeans pocket and jimmied it into the space between two boards. Then he slid them apart and lifted them, exposing an open space.

Hovering over him, Claire gasped. "We're going down there?"

"It's the escape route. Every one of our safe houses has one."

"Why do we need an escape route?" She glanced over her shoulder, her wide eyes taking on the color of the gray smoke billowing around them.

"They're waiting for us."

Her face blanched but she didn't hesitate when he nudged her toward the gaping space in the floor.

"Once through, there should be some steps but then you're going to have to crouch down and probably army crawl." He kissed her forehead. "Can you do that, Claire?"

She nodded and dropped into the hole, the plastic bags crinkling against her chest.

Mike lowered himself after her, dragging his bags with him. He dropped them into the space and then pulled the carpet back over the entrance to the escape route and then reset the planks of wood. Unless Tempest had also gotten the blueprint of the cabin, they wouldn't know where to look.

When he covered the opening, blackness descended on the space around them and Claire trembled beside him.

He flicked on a small but powerful flashlight. "We're good. It's going to be okay."

Two feet into the tunnel they had to drop to their bellies and move single file, pushing their bags in front of them.

Claire choked. "I don't think I can handle this."

"Sure you can, snow queen. Just keep crawling. They're not going to come after us down here."

"But they're waiting for us up there, outside the cabin?"

"That text I got before our world got rocked?

That was Jack warning me that our safe houses along the East Coast had been compromised." He tickled her ankle above her boot. "Keep movin'."

She scrambled forward. "How did that happen?"

"It's the spy business. We get intel on them, and they get intel on us. We have to stay one step ahead of them."

Which he may have done if he hadn't succumbed to his desire for Claire. What had Jack told him? Don't get taken in by the widow's beauty? If it were just her beauty, he could resist.

He'd met a kindred spirit in Claire. Who would've figured a poor boy from the wrong side of the tracks and a society babe would have so much in common? But they'd both been starved for love and had tried to fill that void with other obsessions.

Her gasping breaths filled the tunnel, and he squeezed her foot. "Are you okay? Try not to breathe so heavily."

"Easier said than done. How much farther do we have to go, and where are we going to end up?"

"Not sure, maybe another half a mile. We should wind up right outside that little town."

"How are we going to get out of there? If Tempest agents blew up the cabin and then lay in wait for us outside, once they discover we're not there or not coming out they're going to be watching the bus station."

"You're probably right, which is why we're going to steal a car."

"Are you crazy?"

"We'll make it right—later. Stop talking, save your breath and crawl."

Several feet farther in the tunnel he missed her chatter, but they didn't have enough air in here to be carrying on a conversation, and he didn't want Claire probing his plans too thoroughly. Truth was, in situations like this, it was best not to have too many well-laid plans.

He had no idea if he could find a car to steal or even if there'd be someone waiting for them at the other end of this tunnel.

Claire didn't need to know any of his doubts.

So, they squirmed forward in silence to the beat of their panting breath.

"Mike? I think this is it."

"The end?"

"It looks like solid dirt in front of me and the space opens up a bit."

"Move to the side and I'll squeeze past you."

"This is it. There's a panel of some sort overhead."

"Okay, hang on."

Claire was able to sit up in the space, and his light flicked across her dirt-smudged face.

He clambered beside her and rubbed the dirt from her face with the side of his thumb. "You did great. Almost there."

"Mike?"

"Yeah?" Reaching up he felt along the edges of the panel.

"What if there's someone waiting for us up above?"

He didn't have to tell her his worries. She'd figured them out on her own.

He withdrew his .45 from his pocket and brandished it in the light. "That's why I have this."

He tapped the panel and found an edge. "Stay back, Claire. Get into the farthest corner until I get this thing open and get our bearings."

He pushed against the door and it shifted, allowing a sliver of weak light into their black world. The sun hadn't quite set yet. He pressed his eye to the crack and took in the clearing surrounded by small trees and shrubs. The town lay due east less than half a mile away, and nobody was pointing guns at them—yet.

Shoving the panel aside, he led with his weapon. He poked his head up and sucked in the cold air so fast, it seemed to freeze his lungs. He gulped in a few more frosty breaths.

"It's clear. We're fine."

A small sob escaped from her lips, but she turned it into a cough. "All right, then. Let's get out of this hellhole, and I never meant that statement as literally as I do now."

He climbed up the two steps and stretched out on the ground, cracking his back. Then he rolled over and extended his hands into the opening to help Claire.

She handed him the bags first and then scooted out of the tunnel and collapsed beside him on the frosty ground, breathing heavily.

He inched his hand over and entwined his fingers with hers. "We need to get moving."

"I realize that. I'm just not so sure I can stand up."

He rose to his feet and stomped his boots. "Feels good to be upright."

"Feels good to be alive." She extended her arms, and he took both of her hands and pulled her up until she stood beside him.

"All right. Let's go steal a car."

Forty minutes later, Mike gunned the engine of an old pickup truck and hit the highway heading south.

Claire knotted her fingers in her lap. "Where are we going? I thought all the safe houses had been compromised."

"Do you know Senator Bennett from Connecticut?"

"Not personally."

He steered the truck onto the highway. "I know his son, Jase, and they have a family place in Maryland. We can crash there in between… skulking."

"The senator's not there, is he?"

"The house is empty, except for staff."

Claire shuffled through the glove comportment. "I feel bad about this truck, and it's almost Christmas. What if the guy needs his truck for Christmas?"

"Think of it as a rental. We'll get the truck back to him along with a nice sum of cash. That should brighten his Christmas."

"You're a real Santa." Bending forward, she held the registration up to the little light from the glove box. "Gary Lockhart. He lives in Barnhill, Vermont."

"I'll have someone contact him when we drop the car off at the train station."

"He'll still report the truck as stolen. What if we get pulled over before we get to the station?"

"Then I guess we get booked for car theft, but we won't be in jail for long. It helps to have friends in high places, and we're still not on the FBI's radar." He tapped the radio. "Music? Or do you want to sleep?"

"I slept all day. You must think I'm a slug or something." She rubbed her finger across her teeth. "I could use a toothbrush, though."

"I don't think you're a slug, but our sleep patterns are kind of messed up. That can make you tired no matter how much sleep you get."

She hit the volume button on the radio. "Crank it up."

Static filled the cab of the truck, so he tried a

few other stations. "Nothing but classical coming in. You wanna listen to that?"

"Sure, if it doesn't drive you crazy."

He set the station and put the volume on low for background music. "How are you feeling? Any irritation of your eyes or throat from that smoke?"

"I'm okay." She brushed his forearm. "I noticed the hair on your arms got singed. Are you okay?"

Her touch gave him a thrill. He'd been ready to make love to her all over again when they woke up, but Tempest treated them to fireworks of another kind. And it had to be Tempest. No other organization would've been able to compromise a Prospero safe house. Had agents been sent to destroy all of the safe houses they'd discovered, or did they know he and Claire were in Vermont?

He flicked at the burnt hair on his arm. "I hadn't noticed. There were several fires in the living room when I went to retrieve my laptop and bag."

"Thank God you were able to get them and they weren't destroyed." She jerked her thumb over her shoulder. "Is that the money bag in the back?"

"The money and the weapon bag, so along with the laptop, I got all the essentials out of there." He captured her fingers and brought them to his lips. "And the most essential item of all—you."

Sighing, she scrunched down in her seat. "It's a good thing we did sleep in today. If we'd been in that living room, we could've been injured."

"The way that living room looked? There's no doubt."

She swept some dirt from her jeans and then brushed her hands together. "Whoever killed the director must know who you are now and must know that I'm with you. That firebombing proves that, doesn't it?"

"I agree. I doubt that anyone is after me for any other reason."

"I led them to you."

"Or I led them to you. Does it matter?"

"What I'm wondering is if Spencer went through all the trouble to set me up in the eyes of the FBI, why is he trying to kill me now?"

"It's easier." He squeezed her knee. "Sorry, but it's easier for him to have you killed than to have the FBI bring you in for questioning and start answering all kinds of uncomfortable questions. That is, if those were really FBI agents at the bank."

Her knee bounced beneath his hand. "You mentioned that before. How long has that suspicion been swirling through your brain?"

"Since that Tempest agent tried to abduct you from the station in Philly. If someone really wanted to set you up, those would've been FBI agents waiting for us at the station, not some guy with a gun in the ladies' room. Also, your name was never mentioned in the papers, never mentioned in connection with Hamid."

"I don't know if that makes me feel better or worse. At least I don't need to fear getting recognized at the train station or walking down the street." She sat up and grabbed the edge of the dashboard. "That also means I can call Ethan again without the Chadwicks wondering what's going on, right?"

"Were they expecting your call? You said they had him out all day for snowboarding."

"No, but they won't be surprised by a call. If I call on your phone again, the call can't be traced."

"Let me think about it. First things first."

"My son *is* first."

"I know that." He stroked her hair, littered with specks of dirt, but still soft.

"Okay, so what's first for you?"

"Right now? You."

Leaning against the window of the truck, she turned to face him, her eyes glittering in the low light of the truck. "You don't have to say that."

"I know." He drew a line from her cheek to her chin. "But it's true."

"Well, you don't have to worry about me. I'm fine." She gathered her hair into a ponytail with one hand. "So, what's next?"

"We're going to pay a visit to Fiona."

"Tomorrow? In person?"

"Correll's taking that rich widow to the White House. It's the perfect time to visit Spencer's spurned lover."

"We're going to waltz right into Spencer's office after he's been presumably trying to kill me?"

"Presumably." He held up one finger. "Ever hear of a disguise?"

She planted her palms on either side of her head. "My head is spinning. We're going to Maryland first, though, right? Hiding out in Senator Bennett's house? That makes a lot of sense."

"He won't be there, and you should fit right in. The Bennetts are loaded, too, and that house is staffed with servants. In fact, I'm surprised you don't know Jase Bennett. You two must've traveled in the same circles, although you're a little older than he is."

"Watch it." She punched his shoulder. "Do you think all rich people just sort of hang out together and go to the same schools and the same parties?"

"You mean you don't?"

She stuck out her tongue at him, which gave him all kinds of ideas.

"Hey, as long as the Bennett house has hot and cold running water and a roof, I'm there."

And after several hours and three different modes of transportation, they were there.

The brick colonial house with white siding and dark green shutters gleamed behind a tall gate. Mike had already put the word out, and Jase had facilitated their arrival.

One word from Mike into the intercom and the gates opened as if by magic. A housekeeper greeted them at the front door and didn't even turn up her nose at their appearance, as grungy as they must've looked—and smelled.

"I'm Mrs. Curtis. Mr. Jason phoned ahead. None of the family is in residence, however, and the senator and his wife are in Paris for the holidays."

"We won't be any trouble." Claire hugged her plastic bags to her chest and smiled.

"Mr. Jason indicated that you were to make yourself at home. You can call me via the intercom system in the house if you need anything, or just help yourself. There's food in the kitchen, and there are two rooms at the end of the hall, upstairs to your right, ready for you."

"Thank you, Mrs. Curtis. We can manage." Mike took Claire's arm and steered her upstairs. He whispered in her ear, "Two rooms?"

"I guess you forgot to tell Mr. Jason that you crossed the line between work and pleasure."

He grabbed her hand. "Did I tell you I like the pleasure part a lot better than the work part?"

They stopped at the second-to-last room on the right, and Claire pushed open the door. "This is nice. I think the two rooms are joined by a bathroom."

"You can have the shower first. I need to make a few more phone calls."

She swung her plastic bags in front of her. "The

shower will be great, but I'm afraid I wasn't able to salvage many of the clothes I bought in Vermont."

"Jase has a sister and he said you're welcome to any of her clothes in the house. I don't think she's as tall as you, but she's not short. You should be able to find something to wear."

"And where are we getting our disguises? Not from Jase's sister's closet."

"We'll figure out something." He pulled off his boots and fell across the bed. "When was the last time we ate? My stomach is growling like a hungry bear."

"We had dinner on the way to the city to meet Hamid, unless you had something when we got back to the cabin."

"That was a long time ago. I think a midnight snack is in order even if it's not quite midnight. Should we trouble the accommodating Mrs. Curtis or forage for our own meal in the kitchen?"

"The less contact we have with anyone in this house, the better."

"This is the domain of the Bennett family. Discretion is the word." He held a finger to his lips.

"Yeah, well, you'd be surprised at how much servants talk."

"You mean that loyal retainer stuff is a myth?"

"For some." She shook out some clothes and draped them over her arm. "I'm going to hit the shower. Maybe you can try the kitchen for some food."

"That'd be the first place I'd look."

She rolled her magnificent eyes at him and shut the door of the connecting bathroom behind her.

Mike managed to make it downstairs and find the kitchen without running into another human being in the huge house. He opened the door of the stainless Sub-Zero refrigerator and poked around the containers.

He settled on slicing some cheese, grabbing a few apples and ripping off half a loaf of French bread. He piled his booty onto a big plate and then snagged a bottle of Napa Valley chardonnay from the fridge.

He opened the bottle of wine and shoved the cork back in the top. He carefully threaded his fingers through the stems of two wineglasses, stuffed some paper towels beneath the plate and carried everything back upstairs.

When he entered the room, a cloud of lilac-scented air greeted him, and Claire floated from the bathroom dressed in one of his white T-shirts, toweling her hair dry.

She widened her eyes when she saw him. "Did you clean out the kitchen?"

"Hardly. You should see the stuff they have in there. Those servants must be living it up." He held up the bottle of wine. "Nabbed some good stuff, too."

"Wine? You took a bottle of—" she strolled

toward him and squinted at the label "——what appears to be some very expensive wine?"

He looked at the blue label adorned with a yellow squiggly line through it. "Really? This is expensive?"

She brushed her thumb across the year printed on the label. "I think so."

"Good." He dislodged the cork and poured a measure of the golden liquid into one of the glasses. "You deserve it, and Jase assured me that his casa was our casa, or something like that. Said to take whatever we needed—food, clothing, cars."

"Cars, too?" She took the glass from him and swirled the wine up its sides. "Generous guy, this Jase."

"You got that. He owes me anyway. I've saved his careless ass more times than I can remember."

She took a sip of the wine and closed her eyes. "This is good. That shower was even better."

He set his glass down and peeled off his shirt, crumpling it into a ball. "You eat and I'll get in the shower."

"You said you were starving. Are you sure you don't want to sit down and eat first?" Her fingertips trailed across his pecs and down to his belly, where a fire kindled. "I don't mind that you're... dirty."

He swallowed. "I have a confession to make."

"Really?" She walked her fingers back up his chest and drummed them against his collarbone.

"I already ate a banana downstairs, so I'm not starving anymore." He took her hand and kissed her fingers. "And you're so perfectly fresh and rosy from your shower, I don't want to smudge you."

She lifted her wineglass. "Hurry back…before I eat everything."

He practically ran into the bathroom, unbuttoning his fly on his way. The steam from Claire's shower still fogged the mirror.

He cranked on the water in the stall, big enough to house a family of four, and read the labels on the two bottles of shower gel. At least he didn't need to smell like a lilac.

He squeezed a puddle of fresh ocean breeze into his palm and lathered up. He washed and rinsed his hair, sluicing it back from his forehead as he faced the spray. He almost felt human.

Then he felt superhuman when he walked back into the bedroom with the towel wrapped around his waist and saw Claire sitting cross-legged on the bed biting into an apple.

She said around chews, "You clean up nicely."

"I was thinking the same about you." He ran a hand through his wet hair. "Hard to believe you were crawling through an underground tunnel about six hours ago."

"Hard to believe we made it out alive." She wiped her hands with a paper towel and then rolled up her apple core in it.

He dug into his bag and pulled out a clean pair of boxers. He put them on beneath his towel and then dropped the towel.

Half closing her eyes, she tossed back some wine. "Damn, I was looking forward to the striptease with the towel coming off."

"How many of those glasses have you had?" He sat down next to her on the bed and curled his hand around the neck of the wine bottle, lifting it up to the light.

"Enough." She yawned and fell over on her side, dragging a pillow beneath her cheek.

He smiled and stroked a length of creamy thigh that was exposed as his T-shirt hiked up around her hips. "Can I tempt you with a toothbrush and some toothpaste?"

"Absolutely." She shot up, the thought of brushing her teeth giving her new life. She tumbled from the bed, yanking the T-shirt down around her thighs.

Mike finished off the bread and cheese and had started on another glass of wine by the time Claire stumbled back into the bedroom.

"Ah, such a simple amenity can make all the difference in the world." Running her tongue along her teeth, she fell across the bed. "Did I leave you enough food and drink?"

"Plenty. Are you ready to go back into the fray tomorrow?"

She cocked her head. "By *fray* do you mean go to Spencer's office and try to pump Fiona for information?"

"Exactly."

"It feels dangerous being back here." She folded her arms behind her head. "Back in the vicinity of the political world, close to the White House. What do you think Tempest is going to do?"

"Not sure, but I plan to be in the thick of it to stop them."

"It's important to you, isn't it? I mean, it's important to everyone, but it's personal with you. What happened on your last assignment?"

He choked on the smooth sip of wine trailing down his throat. Even slightly tipsy, she could read him. "Who says anything happened on my last assignment?"

"You don't have to tell me if you don't want to, Mike, but it's so clear that things didn't end well for you. This White House plot fell into your lap, a way to redeem yourself."

"No wonder you had Spencer Correll figured out. You're one perceptive lady."

When it didn't involve her own motives.

"I just understand that drive to prove yourself."

He tossed back the rest of the wine in one gulp. "Okay, my previous assignment didn't have the ending I wanted. We lost hostages. I'd never lost hostages before."

"It happens." She stared past him into the space over her shoulder. "Those situations are chaotic and dangerous. I'm sure it wasn't your fault."

"I was leading the charge, so to speak."

"Nobody else blamed you, did they? Jack didn't blame you."

"I blamed me." He pushed off the bed and collected the dishes. "Do you want anything else from downstairs? Water?"

"Yes, water, please." She waved her hand up and down his body. "Are you venturing out in your boxers? You might give Mrs. Curtis a fright...or the thrill of a lifetime."

His lips twisted. "I suppose I'd better pull on some sweats."

"Chicken."

He left the wine and took everything back downstairs. Again, silence greeted his presence. He stayed in the kitchen for several minutes, throwing away their trash and washing the plate and glasses.

By the time he crept upstairs with a couple of bottles of water tucked beneath his arm, Claire was curled up on the bed, her hand beneath her cheek and her damp hair fanning out on the pillow.

Any thoughts he'd had of making wild, passionate love to her ended on a sigh from her lips.

He drowned his disappointment by gulping down the rest of the wine straight from the bottle—the only way to drink the good stuff.

He then brushed his own teeth and killed the lights in the room. Tugging on the covers, he nudged Claire's body aside and then pulled the covers over her, tucking them beneath her chin.

He yanked off his sweats and crawled into the bed beside her. Crossing his arms beneath his head, he peered through the darkness at the ceiling.

They had to get something on Spencer Correll, and if he was involved with Tempest, he'd get the details of the White House Christmas Day plot out of him one way or another.

Mike let out a long, slow breath. Two days until Christmas…two days until redemption.

CLAIRE LAID A line of kisses down the length of Mike's very long back. If she thought she could slowly awaken him with her kisses, she had the wrong spy.

He turned to face her with a suddenness that had her gasping for breath, her lips against his stomach.

Plowing his fingers through her hair, he growled, "Did you think you could toy with me?"

"A girl can hope." She flicked her tongue against his bare skin and he sucked in a sharp breath.

"You fell asleep last night before I got back from the kitchen. I thought I'd lost my touch."

She rolled up the T-shirt, baring her breasts to his hungry gaze. "So, touch and let's see if you lost it."

Before the last word left her lips, Mike pounced on her and made thorough love to every inch of her body.

They showered again—together this time—and then raided Jase's sister's closet.

Claire fingered the silk Prada jacket. "Nice stuff, but if I'm going to be someone else and try to blend in, I'd better not wear flashy clothing like this."

Mike jerked open another closet door. "We have the cold weather on our side. Jackets, scarves, hats—just like you dressed up when we went into that town in Vermont. We even have the sun out today to warrant a big pair of sunglasses."

Claire dangled a pair of black leggings from her fingers. "I can wear these with the boots I bought in Vermont, pile on a long sweater with a scarf, hat and sunglasses. It's not like Spencer's going to be on the lookout for me, right?"

"Right. Maybe we can avoid the office altogether. Is there someplace you can meet Fiona outside the building?"

"There are a couple of cafés on the street,

although they're frequented by a lot of politicians. I'd hate to have to hide in plain sight with someone I know looking at me."

"Most of those politicians are out of town for the recess." Mike yanked a long blue coat from a hanger and held it up. "Is there any place Fiona goes at lunchtime? Does she get her nails done?"

"I know." Claire dropped the leggings. "Fiona goes to a psychic in the area."

"Like to get her fortune told? Do people really do that?"

"I think it's tarot cards and astrological charts, and Fiona's been seeing this psychic, Madam Rosalee, for a while. She was going on and on about the psychic when she gave me Spencer's password, about how Madam Rosalee had predicted the end of her relationship."

Mike shrugged. "It takes all types. Do you think Fiona will meet you there?"

"I'll talk to Madam Rosalee first and have her get Fiona down there on her lunch hour."

"I'm assuming you'll need some money to make that happen?"

Claire rubbed her thumb across the tips of the rest of her fingers. "I'm going to need money for all of it."

"That I have." Mike tossed the coat at her. "I don't have to be there, but I'll be nearby. You know what to ask Fiona, right?"

"If she knows anything suspicious about my stepfather and if she's willing to spill."

"Let's do this."

Mike borrowed the least flashy car in the Bennett stable—a black Mercedes sedan—and drove them back to DC.

He had his own disguise, as he'd let his beard grow out and now sported a substantial scruff, liberally streaked with gray. Before they left the house that morning, he'd also cropped his longish black hair and then shaved his head down to a stubble.

Claire stole a sideways glance at him in the driver's seat of the car and clicked her tongue. She'd loved the way that long lock of hair had fallen over one of his eyes, but the shaved head and beard gave him a decidedly dangerous look.

"Why are you clicking your tongue at me?"

"I sort of liked your shaggy hair."

He ran a hand over his scalp. "Good disguise, though, right?"

"It makes you look…different for sure, kind of lethal." She stuffed her hair beneath her hat. "Do I look different enough?"

"It's hard to tell what you look like since you're all covered up, but then so is everyone else in this cold spell we're having."

She directed him to Madam Rosalee's and he laughed every time she said the psychic's name.

"Stop." She smacked his thigh. "It's as good a name as any for a psychic."

"Do you believe in that stuff?"

"No, but that doesn't matter. Fiona does, and I know she'll jump at the chance to see Madam Rosalee, especially now that she's on the outs with Spencer."

She pointed out the psychic's small blue, clapboard house between two office buildings. The sign on the house sported a yellow hand with the words *Psychic Readings* in squiggly blue script in the middle of it.

Mike dropped her off in front and went looking for parking.

Claire cupped her hand over her eyes as she peeked in the window. She saw no one, so she opened the door and a bell tinkled her arrival.

The smell of sandalwood incense permeated the air, and a few shelves contained decks of tarot cards, more incense, candles and other psychic accoutrements.

Claire called out, "Hello? Madam Rosalee?"

A beaded curtain clicked and clacked and an enormous woman bedecked in flowing scarves and a green peasant skirt threaded with gold emerged into the room.

Claire pressed her lips together to vanquish her smile. Mike would've gotten a kick out of the cliché that was Madam Rosalee.

Madam Rosalee stopped and spread her arms,

closing her eyes. "I sense an aura of danger. Are you safe?"

The smile on Claire's lips died and she crossed her arms over her chest. "Yes, I'm safe. I didn't come here for myself."

"They never do." Madam Rosalee's heavily lined eyes flew open. "What can I help you with?"

"I need to talk with one of your clients, on the sly, and I thought this might be a good place to do it."

"Why would I lure one of my clients here on a false premise?"

"I'll give you m-money." Claire faltered at the look from Madam Rosalee's dark, slitted eyes.

"You think you can come into my establishment and give me money to get one of my clients here so you can ambush him or her?"

"I'm sorry." Claire blew out a breath. Would Mike have been able to handle this any better? "It's really very important. It's crucial that I talk with her. I can't go to her office and I'm afraid to meet her in public."

Afraid? Where had that come from?

Madam Rosalee held up one pudgy finger with an extremely long red nail on the end and a ring that snaked over her first knuckle.

"You're afraid to meet her in public?"

"Yes. Yes, I am." Claire held her breath.

"Then this is related to the danger and fear that are coming off of you in waves."

"It must be. I guess it is." Who said Madam Rosalee was a fake?

"I don't want your money."

"Is that a refusal? I'm begging you, really, to contact Fiona Levesque. I need to talk to her. Sh-she may be in danger, too."

"I don't want money, but you'll give me something else."

"Anything, just ask and I'll get it for you."

Madam Rosalee approached her slowly and circled her, waving her silky scarves around Claire's body. Claire felt as if she'd landed in the middle of someone's magic show.

"What? What do you want?"

Madame Rosalee trailed a scented scarf over Claire's head. "I want to do a reading for you."

Chapter Thirteen

Claire's shoulders sagged. She'd almost expected Rosalee to ask for her firstborn child. "Of course, if that's all you want. But can we hurry so we can get Fiona here on her lunch hour?"

"I'll take care of that right now." She picked up her cell phone and gestured to the small table covered with a black velvet cloth. "Sit."

Claire took a seat at the table, stroking the soft velvet with her fingertips, and listened to Madam Rosalee's call to Fiona.

"Yes, something very important, my dear. Your very life could depend on it." She ended the call and placed her phone on the shelf next to the small table. "Fiona will be here just after noon. Are you ready?"

"As ready as I'll ever be." Claire folded her hands on the table and gave Madam Rosalee a tight, polite smile.

"Have you ever had a tarot reading before?"

"No."

"Your name?" Madam Rosalee settled her

massive girth into the winged-back chair across from her.

"Claire." She glanced over her shoulder at the window. Had Mike expected her to come outside once she'd convinced Madam Rosalee to set up the meeting with Fiona?

As if she'd summoned him with one of Madam Rosalee's charms, Mike burst through the door of the shop, sending the little bell into a tizzy.

His arrival didn't disturb Madam Rosalee at all, maybe so she could make the claim that she'd expected him to show up all along.

She lifted an eyebrow. "Are you with Claire?"

"Yeah, what's going on?" He dropped a hand to Claire's shoulder. "I was worried about you."

Madame Rosalee nodded. "Could you please turn around the sign at the door and lock it?"

"Claire?" He put pressure on her shoulder.

"Madam Rosalee's payment for luring Fiona over here is a tarot reading for me."

"Is that okay with you?"

She patted his hand still resting on her shoulder. "It's a tarot reading, Mike. Go switch the sign at the door and lock it."

"I'm not going anywhere." He stepped back and locked the door while flipping the sign over to read Closed to the outside world.

"Nobody's asking you to, Mike, as long as you sit quietly during the reading." Madam Rosalee handled a deck of tarot cards, the heavy rings flashing on her fleshy hands.

Mike shrugged at Claire and took a seat in the corner of the room.

Madam Rosalee turned over a row of cards in the middle of the table, tapping them, changing their position, crossing one over another.

The colorful figures and symbols meant nothing to Claire, but the atmosphere in the room grew heavy with anticipation.

After several minutes Madam Rosalee finally spoke. "You are in danger, but we'd already established that."

Mike shifted forward in his seat, and Claire threw a glance his way.

Claire cleared her throat. "Is the danger imminent or vague?"

"It's imminent."

"Avoidable?"

"It's avoidable as long as you aren't alone. On your own, the black sword of death hangs over your head."

Claire rolled her shoulders. That made sense for anyone.

"Love," Madame Rosalee said as she tapped a card, "and death. The two are linked for you and have been for some time."

Claire covered her mouth with one hand. "That was true in the past. Is it true in the future?"

"Just as in the past, in the future and for all

time, if love is strong enough, it can vanquish the danger."

Madam Rosalee droned on about money and family, but nothing she said could replace the uneasiness in the pit of Claire's stomach.

Love? Mike didn't love her. They'd had a connection and some great sex, but that didn't equal love—at least not a love great enough to vanquish the evil they faced.

Madame Rosalee gathered her cards and pushed up from her chair. "I'll be in the back to give you some time to talk to Fiona."

The disappearance of her large presence seemed to suck the life and the drama out of the room.

Mike got up and stretched. "Pretty generic stuff, huh?"

"Yes, yes, of course."

"Why did she want to tell your fortune?" He peered out the curtains at the front window and unlocked the door.

"I'm not sure. As soon as I walked in, she sensed the danger of my aura."

He turned and grabbed her around the waist. "As soon as I saw you, I sensed the sexiness of your aura." He nuzzled her neck.

Leaning back in his arms, she rubbed her knuckles across the black stubble on his head. Annoyance niggled at the edges of her mind. Madam Rosalee had just been telling her how love could stave off the danger, and all Mike could think about was sex.

He blinked his dark eyes, the lusty gleam dimming. "I'm sorry. The palm reading really upset you."

"It was a tarot card reading."

"That's what I meant." He released her and returned to the window. "Fiona's coming at noon?"

She swallowed the lump in her throat. She'd better prepare herself for Mike's departure as soon as he single-handedly saved the White House. And if he couldn't single-handedly save the White House? He'd be unbearable company anyway.

"A little after, I think."

"Is Fiona a busty redhead with a little wiggle in her walk?"

She snorted. "I suppose a man would describe her that way."

"She's here in three...two...one."

The bell on the door jingled and Fiona poked her head into the room. "Madam Rosalee?"

Claire plucked the hat from her head and shook out her hair. "It's me, Fiona. It's Claire Chadwick."

"Claire?" Fiona covered her mouth. "What are you doing here? Are you okay?"

"Okay? Why wouldn't I be okay? What story is Spencer floating around town about me?"

"Spencer." Fiona spit out his name, which was all kinds of wonderful. "Is he spreading lies about you? I wouldn't doubt that for a minute."

"What's he saying, Fiona?" Mike wedged a shoulder against the wall.

"Who's this tall drink of water?" Fiona batted her lashes. "Oh, wait. Are you Mitch, the fiancé?"

"Sort of. What's Senator Correll been saying about us?"

Fiona flipped back her red hair. "Am I here to meet you? Is Madam Rosalee even here?"

"She's here." Claire tugged on Fiona's scarf. "I'm sorry, Fiona. She helped me get you here. I need your help."

"The same way I helped you before?"

"Yes."

"I don't know, Claire. I think Spencer found out about the last time."

Claire's heart skipped a beat. "How? You didn't tell him?"

"Me?" Fiona's voice squeaked. "I value my life too much. Trey figured something out. Spencer had him look at his office laptop because someone kept sending him emails with photos and videos. I think Trey figured out that Spencer was just dragging them into his trash can without doing a hard delete on them. While Trey was helping him, he figured out that someone had viewed a video from the trash."

"That's probably when he started tracking you, Claire." Mike paced the small room. "Maybe that's when he formed his plan against you, also."

He landed in front of Fiona, towering over her

petite frame. "You still didn't tell us. What's Spencer saying about Claire? How's he explaining her disappearance?"

Fiona took a step back, and Claire tugged on Mike's coat. "Don't scare her. She's not the enemy."

"Enemy?" Fiona flipped up the lapels of her coat. "There's an enemy here? I thought this was some kind of dispute between you and your stepfather over money."

"It is, and other stuff."

"Well…" Fiona glanced at Mike, who had returned to the window and stuffed his hand into his pocket. "Spencer is implying that you've had another breakdown."

Claire cursed. "That's almost worse than being wanted by the FBI."

"Wanted by the FBI?" Fiona's blue eyes got round as she shook her head. "He's not saying that. He said Director Haywood's murder in front of your house shook you up so much, you started making wild accusations and your fiancé had to take you away."

"So, I can walk back into my own house right now without fear of being taken into custody?"

Fiona lifted a shoulder. "I don't know anything about that, Claire. You know the man they suspected of putting the car bomb on the director's car is dead?"

Claire and Mike exchanged a quick glance. "Hamid Khan."

"That's right. They're calling him a lone wolf."

Mike coughed. "A lone wolf who poisoned himself?"

"I don't know all the details." Fiona waved her hands. "I just know he's dead and we're supposedly out of danger, but I can't wait to get out of this city. It's Christmas Eve tomorrow, and I'm outta here."

"Can you help us before you leave, Fiona?" Claire held out the envelope of cash she'd been ready to give Madam Rosalee. "I'll make it worth your while."

"I'll take it, but it's just icing on the cake. Do you know that SOB is taking that rich widow to the White House on Christmas Day? If he thinks he's going to squire her around in public during the day and end up in my bed at night, he's dreaming."

Claire suppressed a shiver of revulsion at the thought of Spencer Correll in bed with anyone. "He's a pig, Fiona. Do you have anything you can give us to use against him?"

"I told you, someone keeps sending him emails with videos and pictures. It freaks him out. I don't know if it's blackmail or what."

Mike asked, "Has he gotten any lately?"

"He gets something almost every day."

Claire clasped her hands in front of her. "Can you get them out, Fiona?"

Fiona tilted her red head. "Why don't you come and get it yourself? It's the day before Christmas Eve. There's hardly anyone in the office. Spencer is busy with God knows what. He told me not to expect him in the office until after the break."

Mike shook his head. "Claire, he might be monitoring the office. He might have eyes and ears there. It's too risky."

"I don't like what I'm hearing." Fiona shoved the envelope of money into her purse. "Why would Spencer be watching for you, Claire? And what's he going to do if you show up?"

"If I give you a thumb drive, Fiona, can you copy Spencer's emails to it?"

"I can do that." Fiona skimmed her nails along the velvet cloth covering Madam Rosalee's tarot reading table. "But this is my last day in the office until after New Year's. How am I going to get it back to you?"

"Do you still get off at five?"

"Yeah."

"Mike?" Claire turned toward him.

He scratched his beard. "How do you get to work, a car or public transportation?"

"I take a bus. The stop is a block down from the office."

"We'll be waiting on the street in front of the office when you get off—black Mercedes sedan.

Hand the drive to Claire through the window and have a happy holiday."

Claire pressed the thumb drive into Fiona's hand, and she dropped it into her purse.

"What if there's nothing in the emails?" Fiona clutched her bag to her chest. "Do I still get to keep the money?"

"Absolutely. I appreciate this so much. You have no idea." She gave Fiona a one-armed hug.

As Fiona opened the front door and set off the bells, Rosalee swept aside the beaded curtain and pointed at her. "Be careful. The aura of danger is strong."

WHEN THEY LEFT Madam Rosalee's, Mike headed a few miles outside the city center where he drove through a fast-food place.

They parked in the lot and Mike wolfed down a couple of burgers while Claire sipped on soda.

Between bites, he said, "I am so done with this. If I go through one fast-food place when I retire, that'll be one too many."

Claire chewed on the end of her straw. "I hope Spencer still has some of those incriminating photos in his email. Who do you think is blackmailing him?"

"It could be anyone. It could be Caliban himself. Once you start playing games like Correll, you're in bed with some very dangerous people."

His phone buzzed and Claire jumped. She'd

called her son this morning and had given Ethan's grandparents this number to call in case of an emergency.

Cupping the phone in his hand, he glanced at the display and shook his head at Claire. "It's Jack."

He pushed the button to answer. "I'm still alive, in case you're wondering, oh, and you're on speaker. Claire's in the car."

"Good. You both need to hear this."

Claire bolted upright in her seat. "The videos?"

"We've identified the Oxford Don, Claire. Donald Yousef is the one who executed your husband and he's the one in the video with Senator Correll."

A sob broke from Claire's throat and she covered her face with her hands.

Mike rubbed her back. "Do you know where he is, Jack?"

"He's somewhere in the States. He's a British citizen on a visit and has overstayed his welcome."

"So, he could be here in DC."

"He could be anywhere."

Claire sniffled. "Is this enough to move in on Correll, Jack?"

"We have no audio from the video, no way of knowing why or how he met Yousef. He could claim it was a chance meeting or that Yousef contacted him and he had no idea who he was."

Mike slammed his hands against the steering

wheel. "But it's gotta be enough to bring Correll in for questioning, to start an investigation."

"It is, and we're working on it right now. Are you two safe?"

"Safe and working on a new lead on Correll. Anything on the White House plot?" Mike held his breath. He wanted in on that in the worst way.

"We've notified White House security and the CIA that there's a credible threat against the White House on Christmas Day. They're sweeping the buildings and the grounds, including the room where the memorial for Haywood is being held. They haven't come up with anything, and that room has been sealed off since the sweep—nobody in or out."

"Then it's a threat from the outside in. Correll must know about the extra security precautions."

"He does."

"I wonder if he realizes that Mike and I are behind them." Claire brushed her wet cheeks.

"He just might, Claire. That's why you two still need to keep a low profile."

Mike crumpled up the paper from his burgers. "Is sitting in a fast-food parking lot in Virginia low profile enough?"

"Figures you'd be eating, Becker. Just so you know, Bennett and Liam McCabe are heading out to DC to work this White House threat."

Mike closed his eyes briefly as a shaft of pain knifed his temple. "Sure, boss."

Jack paused. "Mike, you've been my number-one guy for a long time and you're number one on this assignment, too. You have nothing to prove."

"Got it, boss. Keep me posted."

"Same atcha."

Mike ended the call and then curled his arm around Claire, pulling her close. "You did it, snow queen. Justice for Shane. How does it feel?"

She blinked wet lashes at him. "Like some huge weight off my shoulders, like I can move forward with my life."

"You're not going to shift your focus back to your mother's accident?"

"If Prospero or the CIA can link Spencer to these terrorists, to Tempest, and put him away? That's justice for Mom, too."

He kissed the side of her head. "Maybe Fiona can give us something that'll put the nail in Correll's coffin, and then he'll give it up on the White House plot and Caliban."

"It's good that Prospero is sending backup, right?" She entwined her fingers with his. "The point is to stop the attack. You'll still be in on the action."

"Of course." He squeezed her hand, cursing his transparency in her presence. "It's almost five o'clock. Let's go meet Fiona."

They drove back to DC and through the crowded streets near the Mall with Claire directing him toward her stepfather's office building.

As they turned the corner, Mike's hands tightened on the steering wheel. An ambulance, fire truck and three Metro police cars took up the space on the curb in front of a high-rise office building.

"Is that his building, Claire?"

She had one hand at her slender throat. "Yes. It can't be… Please, God."

Mike slowed the car as he pulled up behind a fire truck parked at an angle. He rolled down the window and shouted to a guy at the edge of a crowd of people on the sidewalk. "What's going on? What happened?"

The man took a step back from the crowd. "Some woman. Someone said she was attacked in that stairwell in the parking structure."

Claire hung on the edge of the car window. "Is she okay?"

"No idea. I think they're putting her on a stretcher now."

Mike threw the car into Park. "Climb into the driver's seat in case you have to move the car. I'm going to have a look."

He jumped out of the car and shouldered his way through the crowd, peering over everyone's head. The EMTs raised the gurney and started wheeling it toward the open doors of the ambulance. A white sheet was pulled up to a woman's chin, but not over her face. Mike's gut knotted when a tumble of red curls spilled over the side of the gurney.

With his heart thudding in his chest, he made his way back to the illegally parked car with Claire in the driver's seat, her head bowed.

He slid into the car next to her and slammed the car door. Punching his fist into his palm, he swore. "Damn. It's Fiona. She looks badly beaten, but she's not dead. Thank God, she's not dead."

Claire put the car in gear and squealed away from the curb, glancing over her shoulder.

She took the next turn hard and then gunned the sedan on the straightaway.

"Claire?" Mike drew his eyebrows over his nose. "Are you okay? It was Fiona on that stretcher."

"I know." She plunged her hand into the cup holder and swung a thumb drive from its ribbon. "But we got the goods anyway."

Chapter Fourteen

Mike snatched the drive from her fingers. "How the hell did you get this?"

"While you were on the sidewalk, Madam Rosalee came up to the car window and gave it to me."

"Madam Rosalee?" He drove the heel of his hand against his forehead. "Now I'm really confused."

"She didn't have much time to talk. You can imagine she wanted to get out of there, but she told me she'd had a bad feeling about Fiona when she left her place—that dangerous aura."

"Yeah, or maybe she just eavesdropped on our conversation."

"Whatever." Claire flicked her fingers in the air. "She went to Fiona's office on the pretense of delivering her astrological chart and told her that if she hung on to that thumb drive I gave her, she'd be in mortal danger. She assured Fiona she'd get the drive to me.

"Fiona told her to give it to us when we pulled

up to the curb, that she'd wanted to leave the office early anyway since it was her last day before the holidays. Madame Rosalee stopped for coffee to wait for us when all the commotion started. Someone had discovered Fiona in the stairwell, beaten to a pulp, and called 9-1-1."

"My God. They knew. Somehow they knew Fiona had taken that info. Maybe Trey Jensen placed a tracer on Correll's computer." He made a fist around the thumb drive. "But we got the info anyway."

Claire bit her lip. "Whoever beat up Fiona didn't find anything on her. They might believe they were mistaken."

"I doubt it, Claire. They know she took something, and they may know that we have it. I just hope to God she pulls through."

"H-how did she look?"

"Bad, had an oxygen mask over her face, but I didn't hear anything about her getting shot or knifed."

"Thank God for small favors." She huffed out a breath. "After what Fiona paid to get this out, I hope there's something on it we can use to nail Spencer for sure."

"So do I. I'm also hoping there's something about the Christmas Day attack. We need all the help we can get on that." He tapped the GPS on the car's control panel. "Do you know the way back to the Bennetts'?"

"I have a terrible sense of direction. Punch it in."

Mike entered the address into the GPS and checked his watch. "We'll check on Fiona later when they get her to the hospital."

The voice on the GPS directed her to take the next turn, and Claire turned down the volume. "Do you think she told her attacker about the thumb drive? About us?"

"Fiona is a pampered admin assistant in a senator's office." Mike traced the edges of the thumb drive. "I think she told them everything and would've given up the drive if she'd had it on her, and I don't blame her for it at all."

Claire squeezed her fingers around the steering wheel as a sick feeling seized her gut. "But she didn't tell them about Madam Rosalee, or they would've gone after her. She didn't tell them about the handoff at five o'clock or we would've seen someone—emergency vehicles or no emergency vehicles."

"My guess is she told her assailant that she already gave the drive to us. At that point, she could assume Madam Rosalee would be successful in putting the drive in our hands."

"Once Spencer goes down, I'll make sure Fiona gets another job on The Hill if she wants it." Claire ground her back teeth together. If Spencer could arrange for his former lover to get beaten, who knew what else he'd be capable of doing?

"That would be a hard sell."

"What would?"

"Finding a position for someone in government who'd sell out her boss for a few bucks."

"Ah, but she didn't sell out her boss. She was assisting in the takedown of a terrorist."

"Let's hope she survives to take advantage of your salesmanship."

They drove in silence for the next several miles, during which time Claire said a number of prayers for Fiona and even a few for Madam Rosalee.

They crossed into Maryland and Claire asked, "Is Jase going to be at his house when we get there?"

"I'm not sure. He's been with his fiancée, who's expecting a baby. She's been through a tough time, so I'm surprised Jack got him to come out here, although Jase probably jumped at the chance to take down a Tempest plot."

"He has history with Tempest, too?"

"Yeah, Liam and Jase—and now me."

Another few miles and Claire pulled the sedan up to the Bennett fortress. Mrs. Curtis had given them the code for the gate, and Claire entered it.

Mrs. Curtis met them at the front door, her eyes popping at Mike's altered appearance. She hadn't seen him since they first arrived.

"It's me." Mike skimmed his hand over his buzz cut. "Do you mind if Claire gets some lunch from the kitchen?"

"Of course not. I'm sure Mr. Jason told you to

make yourselves at home. There's cold chicken, some salad and some hummus and pita bread."

Claire plucked the hat from her head. "That sounds good, but, Mike..."

He took her by the shoulders and aimed her in the direction of the kitchen. "Eat. I'll bring my laptop into the kitchen and we can multitask."

Mrs. Curtis bustled ahead of her, but Claire put a hand on her back. "Don't go to any trouble, Mrs. Curtis. I can help myself."

"I'll just take it out for you, and then I'll leave you two alone to discuss business."

How did she know they had business to discuss? Must be all those years looking after Mr. Jason.

Mrs. Curtis puttered around the kitchen, unwrapping some chicken and popping a few rounds of pita bread into the microwave. "Would you or Mr. Becker like some coffee?"

"I wouldn't, not sure about Mr. Becker."

Mike barreled back into the kitchen, his laptop tucked beneath his arm, "Not sure about what?"

"Would you like some coffee, sir?" Mrs. Curtis held up the coffeepot.

"No, thanks."

"Then I'll leave you two." Mrs. Curtis stopped at the door. "Only Mr. Curtis and I are in residence, in the back house, and we're leaving for Mississippi later tonight to visit our grandchildren for Christmas."

Mike issued a mock salute. "Thanks for everything, Mrs. Curtis, and enjoy your holiday. We'll be fine on our own, and Jase is due back tonight or tomorrow morning."

She smiled and wished them a merry Christmas, then headed out the side door toward the back house on the grounds.

Mike set up his laptop on the granite island in the middle of the kitchen while Claire spooned some hummus onto a plate. She removed the pita from the microwave and tore off a piece.

Mike looked up from his computer. "Jack sent me the file they have on Donald Yousef, and it's not much."

Clicking the keyboard to scroll through the file, he continued, "He's been keeping a low profile. He's not on any watch lists, hasn't attended any training camps that we know of. There's been no indication in the past that he's been involved in terrorist activity."

"But Prospero is still sure he's the man in the video with Shane?"

"They've verified it through some very sophisticated computer matching of features, body type, gestures."

"Will that hold up if they decide to pick him up and detain him for questioning?"

"The system we're using is not recognized in court, but for us it's enough to bring him in—when we locate him."

He tapped the keyboard a few more times and then frowned.

"What's wrong? You look confused."

"Who's that woman your stepfather is taking to the White House event? Brit-Saud Oil, right?"

"That's right." She licked some hummus from her fingers. "Julie Patrick. Her husband owned massive shares of Brit-Saud Oil, and now they're all hers."

"Brit-Saud Oil." Mike tapped his finger against the laptop's screen. "Don Yousef is a beneficiary of Brit-Saud Oil."

Her heart jumped. "What does that mean, *beneficiary*?"

"The company offers scholarships to promising students in the Middle East who have been adversely affected by war."

"Is that how Yousef got to Oxford?"

"Yes, and you'll never guess who's chairperson of that program."

Claire dropped her pita bread on the counter. "Julie Patrick?"

"Exactly." He hunched over the laptop. "Where did you read that puff piece about the guest list for the director's memorial?"

"The *Washington Spy.*"

"That's appropriate." He brought up the website and did a search for the article. "This only mentions Correll and his guest, Julie Patrick. We need to get ahold of that guest list."

"If Prospero is monitoring security at the White House for the event, they'd have the guest list, right?"

"Yep." Mike had already lunged for his phone. "Jack, I need that guest list for the Haywood memorial. More specifically, is Julie Patrick bringing a guest?"

Jack's voice came over the phone's speaker. "Hang on. Do you want me to send it to you or just tell you over the phone?"

"I just need to know if she's bringing a guest— over the phone."

Jack paused and then came back on the line. "Julie Patrick is most definitely bringing a guest."

"Who is it, Jack?" Claire gripped the edge of her stool. "Is it Donald Yousef?"

"Donald Yousef? Of course not. After ID'ing him as your husband's executioner, you don't think we'd notice his name on the White House guest list?"

Mike held up his index finger at Claire. "Then who is it, Jack? Who's she bringing?"

"Some kid named Assad Ali-Watkins. He's one of her scholarship kids."

Claire jumped off her stool and shouted into the phone, "Jack, it's him. He's the threat."

"What's she talking about, Mike?"

"Donald Yousef was one of those Brit-Saud scholarship recipients, too. There's a good chance that Julie Patrick is working to help identify possible recruits for Tempest through this program. The kid is clean, right? He's going to pass any background and he's presumably already been vetted by Brit-Saud Oil."

"Son of a bitch. What are you thinking? Suicide vest?"

"That's exactly what I'm thinking, and if he sees White House security doing a pat-down of dignitaries before they enter the reception, he's going to know something's off and he'll detonate right there or take off."

"We'll have to head him off before he gets to that point. *You'll* have to head him off, Mike. This is yours."

Mike glanced at her, his dark eyes gleaming. "We need to be able to tie this Ali-Watkins to Senator Correll."

"Did you get any more info on him?"

Mike grabbed the thumb drive. "We did, but we haven't looked at it yet because we got sidetracked with the dossier you sent on the Oxford Don."

"Well, get on it. I have complete faith in you, Mike."

On that high note, Mike ended the call and grabbed Claire's face, kissing her on the lips. "I think this is it, snow queen."

The pulse in her throat galloped wildly. "Let's see what Fiona got for us."

Mike inserted the thumb drive and double-clicked on it to open it. Several email files popped up, and Mike opened the first one.

Claire's shoulders sagged. "It's an airline's special deals."

"Fiona probably just copied over all his emails. That's okay. She said he'd been getting emails almost daily, so there has to be something here, unless Jensen was deleting them remotely."

Mike's cell phone vibrated on the countertop and he grabbed it, cupping it in his hand.

"Is it Jack again?"

Mike cocked his head. "It's the Chadwicks from Colorado."

Claire put her fingers to her lips. "I hope Ethan didn't have an accident snowboarding. Should I answer it?"

"Let me." He put the phone back on the counter and tapped the screen. "Hello?"

"H-hello? My daughter-in-law, Claire Chadwick, gave me this number to call."

Mike nodded at Claire.

"Nancy, this is Claire. Is Ethan okay?"

"Oh, no, Claire. Ethan is not okay. He's missing."

Chapter Fifteen

Claire's brain went numb for a moment as she shook her head. It was a joke, some kind of joke.

Claire laughed. "Missing? What does that mean?"

Nancy sobbed, "He's gone, Claire. I'm so sorry, but we thought he was safe. He was with Lori in a class and then he was gone. We've had the snow patrol looking for him, but an instructor in another class thinks Ethan walked away with a man."

Claire doubled over, clutching her stomach.

"Claire?" Barry's voice boomed over the phone. "Does this have anything to do with Shane? Tell us this doesn't have anything to do with Shane."

Mike grabbed Claire's hand. "Mr. and Mrs. Chadwick? This is Claire's friend Mike Becker. Have the kidnappers made any demands yet?"

Through her fog, Claire heard Barry respond. "Nothing. The police and the snow patrol are still searching the mountain. They're not convinced it's an abduction—yet."

"Good." Mike squeezed her hand. "Listen to me very carefully. When the kidnapper calls with his terms, he's going to demand that you leave the police out of it. Do what he says. Is Lori there with you?"

Nancy sniffed. "No, she's at the police station."

"Don't tell Lori you talked to me. Got it? Don't even mention my name."

"Why?" Barry coughed. "Who are you? Where's Claire?"

"Barry?" Claire wiped her face. "I'm right here. You can trust Mike. This is more complicated than a simple...kidnapping."

She shuddered, and Mike wrapped his arm around her. "Do what Mike says. Follow the kidnappers' instructions, and don't tell Lori about Mike."

"Mr. Chadwick, I'm going to hang up now so your line is free. My guess is you'll hear something soon, something before the police set up operations at your house and tap your phones. Play along with that."

Nancy's voice quavered. "This has to do with what happened to Shane, doesn't it, Claire? When will it ever end?"

Claire set her jaw and dashed the last tear from her face. "It ends now, Nancy."

IT TOOK HIM thirty minutes and one glass of wine to calm Claire down and to get her shaking to subside. He'd held her close and whispered in her ear while a black dread grew in his gut.

Now anger had replaced Claire's fear, and she paced the kitchen floor as he continued opening emails.

His frustration had him practically breaking the mouse on the next email he clicked. "There has to be something on here or Correll wouldn't have arranged Ethan's abduction."

Claire dug her fingers into her scalp, grabbing her hair by the roots. "I can't believe he'd actually do harm to Ethan. He played grandpa to that boy."

"He's diabolical, Claire. Tempest and Caliban must've promised him something big for his co-operation in this plan—a starring role in the new world order."

"What about Lori?" She clasped her hands behind her neck and tilted back her head. "Do you suspect Lori?"

"There's no way she let Ethan out of her sight when he was in that snowboarding class." He squinted at the next email, an invitation to play a social media game. "I told you that first day. I walked into something between the two of them. I guess she wasn't as unwilling as she pretended to be."

Claire swept up a knife and stabbed a cutting board. "I should've never let him out of my sight.

I should've let this all go and taken him to Colorado myself."

"Hey, you did what you thought was right at the time. You thought you were keeping him safe."

She covered her face with her hands. "It's Christmas Eve tomorrow. He must be so scared."

"I'm sure he's okay right now."

"Right now." Her hands fisted at her sides. "I'll kill Spencer myself if any harm comes to Ethan."

"Wait a minute. This email has an attachment." He double-clicked on the image file and swore. "Bingo—Correll is trying on a suicide vest."

"What?" She tripped over her own feet getting back to him and the laptop. Hovering over his shoulder, she said, "Oh, my God. There he is. That has to be Ali-Watkins next to him, but who sent the picture and why? Who sent him the video of the meeting with Yousef?"

Mike wiped a bead of sweat from his sideburn. "Someone who wants to keep him in line. All of Correll's meetings with these people have been recorded without his knowledge. By sending the videos and pictures, Tempest is making sure he keeps up his end of the bargain—access to the White House and the highest echelons of government."

His cell phone buzzed, and Claire pounced on it. "It's the Chadwicks."

"Hold on." Mike took the phone from here. "Hello?"

Mr. Chadwick's harsh whisper came over the line. "Someone called us. The police aren't here yet and don't know about the communication, and Lori is resting in her room."

"Good. You're on speaker and Claire's listening in. What do they want?"

"It was a man, disguised voice. He told me not to contact the police about the call and to give a message to Claire."

Claire dragged in a shuddering breath. "What's the message, Barry?"

"It's a phone number, Claire. Just a phone number for you to call, and a picture."

"A picture?" Mike's heart thundered in his chest.

"It's Ethan. He's eating something from a bowl, soup or cereal, and he's sitting in front of a TV with the date and time stamped on the screen. It was taken minutes before the call. Ethan's okay. He's okay right now, Claire."

"He'll be fine, Barry. I won't let anything happen to our boy. We won't lose him."

Barry read off the telephone number while Mike entered it into a file on the computer. He told Barry to hold tight and then he ended the call.

"Are you ready?" He spun the computer around to Claire and pushed his phone toward her.

She licked her lips and tapped the number into the phone.

Spencer Correll answered on the first ring. "Yes?"

Claire growled deep in her throat. "Give me my son back, you son of a bitch."

Correll tsked. "First things first, Claire. Return my emails to me."

"You have to know it's too late for that. I can't unsee what I've already seen—you cavorting with terrorists and suicide vests."

He sighed. "Well, I was afraid of that. Why Caliban felt he had to hold a threat over my head is beyond me, and it backfired. So, there's more to my demands."

"Spill. What do you want me to do in exchange for Ethan?"

"Forget about the Christmas Day plot."

She snorted. "Again, too late. You must know about the heightened security surrounding the event."

"I also know your so-called fiancé is a Prospero agent, and he's going to be front and center during the security check. He needs to facilitate the attack by doing nothing."

Mike pinched the bridge of his nose but kept his mouth shut.

"He's going to do his job. You have to know that."

"If the Prospero agent does his job and the

Christmas Day plot doesn't go off as planned or at least close to plan, Ethan dies."

Mike's gaze jumped to Claire's pale face, her violet eyes blazing.

"You wouldn't do that. You wouldn't harm Ethan."

Correll coughed. "I admit a fondness for the boy, but I have a greater fondness for power. After the successful completion of the Christmas Day plot, we'll be in a position to take control. We've been setting up our coup for over a year now. We're ready. And now that I've gotten rid of Caliban, I'm ready for my close-up."

Mike's head jerked up.

"What do you mean you've gotten rid of Caliban? Who's Caliban? You mentioned him before."

"Stop the pretense, Claire." Correll laughed, a short bark of a laugh. "If you've been keeping company with a Prospero agent, you know all about Tempest and Caliban."

"Who is he, and if you got rid of him, how is he still sending these emails to you?"

"Hell if I know. The power of a technology I don't understand. In fact, you know Caliban very well. He was your archnemesis at one time."

As dizziness swept over her, Claire gripped the edge of the counter. "You can't mean CIA director Haywood."

"Believe it or not. I took him out, using one of his own superagents to position myself for the takeover. I didn't want to be forever looking over my shoulder. He doesn't matter anymore. Tell your Prospero agent to back off, or your son dies."

Mike reached out and pinched Claire's chin between his fingers. Her gaze locked on to his and he nodded.

"I'll try, Spencer. All I can do is try."

"You do that, Claire, because if our plot is foiled, Ethan dies, just like his father before him."

Claire squeezed her eyes shut, and a burning fury raced through Mike's veins.

"The Christmas Day plot will go off as planned. You have my word."

"I'd feel more comfortable about your assertion if I didn't already know you for a lying bitch, just like your mother."

"I think you're the one who lied to my mother."

"Oh, I admit to a few fibs, but she told me all her assets would be mine when she passed away. She even got an attorney to lie to me. Imagine that."

"Then I guess you murdered her for nothing."

"Not nothing, Claire, just not everything. Let the plot go as planned or lose your son."

He cut off the call, and Claire buried her head in her arm, her shoulders shaking. "He did it. He killed my mother, and now he's going to kill my son."

"He's not going to kill Ethan."

She rolled her head to the side and stared at

him through red-rimmed eyes. "What's one boy? What's one little boy compared to a plot to destroy the White House and take over the world?"

"I'll save Ethan, Claire. We'll do both. I'll rescue your son and *then* we'll foil the suicide bombing."

"Ethan's in Colorado. How are you going to do both?"

He stood up and stretched, extending his arms to the ceiling. "I'm only going to do one—save Ethan. That's my number-one priority. You're my number-one priority."

And he'd never been surer of anything in his life.

Chapter Sixteen

The red-eye flight landed in Denver at the break of day. Jack had pulled some national security strings to get them on the flight at the last minute, and then he'd delved into Correll's claim that Jerry Haywood had been Caliban.

Mike picked up the four-wheel-drive rental and they took off for the mountain town where the Chadwicks lived. The snowy landscape flew by in a white blur. They'd exchanged one white Christmas for another.

"Are you sure this will work?" Claire trapped her fidgeting hands between her knees. "How do we even know for sure that Lori is involved?"

"Gut feeling, Claire. Something bothered me about her exchange with Correll in the dining room."

"But she doesn't have to tell you anything. They'll kill her if she does. I'm sure she knows that."

"After tomorrow, Tempest will see all its plans come to nothing. Correll won't be in a position to get back at anyone." Mike turned up the defroster and rubbed the inside of the windshield with his fist.

"Will Prospero be able to root out all the Tempest superagents? Or will another Caliban rise in the vacuum?"

"I'm not sure, but the agency will be crippled all the same, and if the CIA under Haywood had been protecting Tempest all this time, that will all come to an end."

"If Lori doesn't talk, if we can't get to Ethan—" Claire traced a pattern on the passenger window "—what happens? You won't be able to stop Jase and Liam from nabbing Ali-Watkins and thwarting the attack…even if you wanted to."

"You're right. That's not even a possibility at this point." He cupped her cold cheek with his hand. "But this will work. Trust me."

"You asked me to trust you when we set out for Vermont."

"And?" He ran his hand down the length of her hair. "How has that worked out for you?"

"Well, I'm still alive, we've been able to tie Spencer to a terrorist plot and Prospero is about to foil that plot, so I guess it was a smart move on my part." Her bottom lip trembled. "But now they have Ethan."

"I'm going to get him back for you, Claire, and when this is over, we can start fresh—both of us."

"You'll head off into the sunset of your retirement, and I'll take Ethan back to Florida and a normal life." The corner of her mouth turned down.

Was it the thought of going their separate ways that made her sad...or something else? He had to find out, not that her answer would change his current plan to rescue Ethan.

"Will that normal life for you and Ethan include that shrine to Shane?" He sucked in a breath and held it.

She jerked her head toward him, her lips forming an *o*. "I—I'm free of that now. As soon as Yousef is captured, I can put that to rest."

"And what if he's never captured? There is that possibility. We have terrorists on watch lists for years sometimes." His jaw ached with tension.

"I'm done, Mike."

"Good, because if you're my priority, I'm going to have to be yours—or at least a close second to Ethan."

"You weren't just saying that back at the Bennetts'? I was afraid..."

"Afraid of what?" He twirled a lock of her hair around his finger.

"That maybe you'd just gotten carried away with the situation."

"The only thing I'm carried away with is you. I love you, Claire. I want you in my life, whatever that life looks like after this."

Covering her mouth with one hand, she closed

her eyes. "You don't know how much I wanted to hear those words from you."

"Sure I do, because I've wanted to hear the same words from you." He held up his hand. "I'm not putting you on the spot. Your focus right now is getting Ethan back, and that's my focus, too, that's my commitment to you."

"I believe you, Mike. I believe you'll get him back."

And that was what he wanted to hear even more than her pronouncements of love. He needed her confidence and faith in him that he could do this. He'd let his Prospero team members bask in the glory of disrupting the Christmas Day plot.

He wanted to rescue Ethan and bask in the glory of a pair of violet eyes.

Almost an hour later, when they turned up the mountain road that led to the Chadwicks', Mike spotted the police car parked on the side of one of the cabins.

He pointed it out to Claire. "I'm guessing that's their place."

"It is. How are we going to play this?"

"You're not going to play anything. You head straight to the Chadwicks and the rest of the family and talk to the police. Leave the rest in my hands."

She nodded. "Got it."

He parked the rental car down the road from the cabin. No need to give Lori a head start.

Their boots crunched on the ground up to the front door and a sheriff's deputy greeted them. "Can I help you?"

A woman with a long gray braid over one shoulder peered around the officer. "This is Ethan's mother. Claire, we didn't expect you so soon."

Claire brushed past the deputy and embraced the older woman in a hug. "Where else would I be?"

The rest of a very large family crowded around Claire, and Mike looked over their heads and locked eyes with Lori.

She nodded, her face flushed, and stayed in the background.

He kept her in his peripheral vision as Claire made the introductions to about twenty family members. It didn't take long for Lori to shuffle toward the back of the cabin and a side door.

Mike broke away from the group hug and followed Lori outside into the chilly afternoon.

She already had her phone in her hand.

In two long strides, Mike was beside her, snatching the phone from her hand. "I don't think so."

She widened her eyes. "Mr. Brown, is there a problem?"

"I'd say so. Where are they holding Ethan?"

Her mouth dropped open, but fear flashed across her face. He could smell it coming off her.

"I-if I knew that, I'd tell the police. I know it's

my fault for not watching him more closely. I'm torn up about it. I can't even face Claire."

"Yeah, I can imagine it would be hard for you to face Claire after what you've done. How much did Senator Correll pay you, or is he promising something else? Marriage?" He laughed. "Get in line, sister. Correll's a man whore. He spreads around whatever he's got to all the ladies. He must own stock in Viagra."

Lori gasped. "I don't know what you're talking about."

He grabbed her arm, pinching it through the slick material of her jacket. "Let's take a walk."

"Wait." She dug her heels into the frozen ground. "I don't want to leave the house."

"I'll bet you don't." He dragged her away from the cabin. "Especially not with me."

"I don't know what you think is going on. I didn't have anything…"

He shoved the muzzle of his gun in her side. "Cut the crap."

She froze, except for one eyelid that twitched and fluttered. "You wouldn't."

"Kill you?"

"You can't kill me."

"Why? Because you can't tell me where Ethan is if you're dead?"

She parted her dry lips, but didn't answer.

He didn't like roughing up or scaring women. Given his past, it was the hardest part of the job for him when required. But sometimes it was required, and for a woman complicit in the kidnapping of a child—Claire's child—it was more than required.

"Who said anything about killing you, Lori?" He prodded her with his gun farther from the cabin and curled his lip. "Do you know who I am? What I do?"

A line of sweat broke out on her upper lip, despite the cold.

"We reserve death for those who are no longer of any use to us." He cinched his fingers around her wrist. "I have something altogether different planned for you."

"I don't—I don't know anything. I don't know where they have him."

He loosened his grip. "But he must still be in the area if Correll plans to release him after the White House blows tomorrow."

Lori tripped. "White House? What are you talking about?"

"I guess Correll saves his truly intimate conversations for like-minded ladies such as Julie Patrick."

Lori's face twisted, giving everything away.

"He's here in the area, isn't he?"

Dropping her chin to her chest, she whispered, "Yes. Spencer told me when Claire handed over what was rightfully his from his marriage he'd release Ethan to me. I—I don't know anything about the White House."

"We'll take that into consideration. Now, you're going to call the people who have Ethan and tell them you need to see him."

Her head came up as if on a string. "How am I going to manage that? I have no reason to see Ethan until he's released."

Mike narrowed his eyes. "His medicine. He has asthma and he's going to need his medicine. If anything happens to him before Correll gets his...money, the whole plan is ruined. Now get back on the phone and put it on speaker."

She took the phone from his fingers as if his touch would burn her and placed the call.

A man answered on the first ring. "What's the problem?"

"The boy—he doesn't have his asthma medication. I need to get it to him."

"Are you crazy?"

She lashed back. "Are you? If anything happens to him before the boss gets what he wants, we're all dead."

"Are they lookin' at you? Are the cops lookin' at you?"

"No, not at all. Nobody suspects me." She raised her eyes to meet Mike's.

The man on the other end of the line sniffed. "I'm giving you these GPS numbers. You just have to put 'em in a GPS and you'll get here, but you better delete 'em after…and wait until dark."

Mike cocked his head. The guy didn't sound like an elite Tempest superagent.

When he read off the GPS coordinates, Lori scribbled them on her palm while Mike committed them to memory.

"You get your ass over here, deliver those meds and get out. I don't want the kid seeing you. He's already yapping about Christmas. I don't wanna hear any more out of him."

"I'll be there around seven o'clock."

When she ended the call, Mike took the phone away from her and tapped it against his chin. "Who are the kidnappers?"

"I don't know. I only talked to him once before."

"Him? One guy?"

"Spencer figured the fewer people involved, the better."

"He's a local? Some local scumbag?"

"He's from Denver. Spencer knew someone who knew someone."

Mike chuckled. "And he thought he could take over the reins from Caliban? Caliban would've used his agents for an assignment like this."

Lori looked at him like he was the crazy one instead of her. "Who's Caliban?"

"The good senator really did keep you in the dark, unless you're lying—but you're not that good of a liar. I sensed something between you and Correll the first morning I was there. Too bad I didn't know enough then to act on it."

She held up her hand. "I have the GPS coordinates."

"Wash your hands." He tapped his head. "I have them right here."

CLAIRE DIDN'T KNOW what Mike had said to Lori but when they returned to the house, Lori couldn't even meet her eyes. Hope surged within Claire.

She didn't have to pretend to be the frantic mother for the police. She *was* that mother, but she had something other frantic kidnap victims' mothers didn't have—six feet four inches of solid man, willing to do anything to get her son back for her, even give up his chance to make himself whole by foiling the biggest plot of his career.

She and Mike couldn't get any time alone together, until the end of the day.

Mike had been sticking to Lori all day like a burr, and while the others gathered in the kitchen to order some pizza, Mike brought Lori over to Claire and one of the police officers.

"Lori agreed to take me out to the mountain where she last saw Ethan. I'd just like to get a visual, and Lori could use some air."

Did Mike really think she'd let him do this on his own?

"I think that's a great idea."

The deputy scratched his chin. "It's going to be dark soon."

"Night skiing on Christmas Eve, right? We're not going to be searching for clues, Officer. I just want to see the area." He pinched Claire's shoulder. "It might be too upsetting for you, Claire."

"I'm going stir-crazy in here. Maybe Ethan just needs to hear my voice. If someone does have him, maybe he's not far from that spot."

"I—I agree with Claire." Lori took Claire's coat from the hook by the door and pressed it into her hands. "And I'd like an opportunity to explain what happened."

With a furrowed brow the deputy's gaze bounced between the three of them. "You're free to do what you like. Be careful, and report anything to us immediately."

"Of course, and you have Lori's phone number if anything happens here."

Mike took her arm and Lori's as he marched them toward the rental car. He stopped at the rear bumper. "You can go back inside now, Claire. Tell him you changed your mind."

"No way. You're going after Ethan now, aren't you? Do you think I'm going to stay here? He's going to need me. What if…?"

"Nothing's going to happen to Ethan. I'll bring him home safely."

"I won't go unless Claire comes along." Lori folded her arms, hunching her shoulders. "Mitch or Mike or whatever the hell his name is pulled a gun on me, threatened me with bodily harm."

Claire put mittened hands over her ears. She didn't want to know how Mike got his results. "I don't care, Lori. It serves you right. I thought you loved Ethan. I thought you cared for him."

Lori sobbed, "I do. Spencer assured me he'd come to no harm."

"No harm? He's been kidnapped by some lethal superagents."

"What?" Lori stepped back.

Mike heaved out a breath. "No, he hasn't, Claire. I guess Correll thought all he'd have to deal with was the local sheriff's department. He hired some dirtbag out of Denver to do the job."

"Oh, my God." Claire's knees weakened and she put a hand against the car to steady herself. "I don't know if that's better or worse."

"Better, much better." Mike unlocked the doors. "Now let's get going and rescue Ethan."

Mike punched some numbers into the GPS and turned to Lori, whom he'd put in the passenger seat beside him. "Does this guy know your car?"

"No. Spencer sent him a picture of me, that's it."

They followed the directions the GPS intoned, which took them deeper into the mountains. From one ridge, Mike pointed out some lights. "That's probably it, nothing else around here."

He parked the car on an access road and said,

"We walk in from here. Claire, you're not coming to the cabin with us. You wait at a distance."

She nodded. She didn't want to upset his plan. She just wanted to be there for Ethan.

"Do you know how to use a gun?" He pulled a second weapon from his coat and held the butt toward her.

"After all we've been through the past few days, I can't believe you're asking me that now." She gripped the handle. "As a matter of fact, I do."

They all exited the car and hiked down the access road with Lori leading the way.

The cabin up ahead played peekaboo with the trees, and Mike took her arm. "You stay right here, behind this tree. Don't go into that cabin. Don't go anywhere near it."

She grabbed his pockets. "Save my little boy."

"That's what I'm here for." He pressed a quick kiss on her mouth and turned, pushing Lori in front of him.

From her hiding place, she heard Lori call out, "It's me. I have the meds."

Claire leaned against the tree, her hair clinging to the bark. Mike must've remembered that she'd told him about Ethan's asthma scare.

What happened next literally flashed before her eyes in a matter of seconds.

A rectangular patch of light appeared, and then Mike crowded the door behind Lori. There was a shout and then a flash and a bang. Another bang and a long, high scream.

Claire's feet sprouted wings and she flew through the trees to reach the cabin. She tripped over Lori, collapsed at the entrance, rocking and whimpering, blood oozing through the fingers she had clamped to her shoulder.

On her hands and knees, Claire crawled through the door and cried out when her hand met the boot of a man lying on the floor, a puddle of blood beneath his head.

Then her gaze locked on to the tall man in the center of the room, cradling her son in his arms.

Crying out, she launched to her feet and threw herself at both of them. She wrapped her arms around Mike and rested her head against Ethan's legs.

"Mommy?"

"I'm right here, Ethan. Are you okay?"

"I'm okay." He rubbed his sleepy eyes and yanked on Mike's beard. "Mommy, is this Santa?"

"Yes, baby." She pressed her lips against the back of Mike's hand. "This is our Santa."

Epilogue

"Dude, you really didn't miss that much. Ali-Watkins got out of the limo and we swarmed him, dragged him to the staging area we'd set up and disarmed him—or de-vested him."

Mike narrowed his eyes at the young agent, Liam McCabe, stuffing a shrimp puff into his mouth. "Why do people of your generation feel it necessary to call everyone *dude*?"

Claire grabbed Mike's hand. "You're becoming the crotchety old retiree already. Watch yourself."

"Just trying to make you feel better about missing the takedown, du… Mike." Liam pointed to the TV, where Ethan was sitting with Jack and Lola's older son, Eddie, and their twins. "Hey, hey, that's Katie's game."

"What do you mean?" Claire left Mike's side and sauntered up behind the kids. She tousled Ethan's hair as she took in the cartoonish images of the video game playing out across the screen. "How is this Katie's game?"

"She designed it." Liam hung his arm around

the shoulders of his girlfriend and kissed the side of her head. "She's a computer whiz, and that's why I got Jack to hire her at Prospero."

"Really?" Claire smiled at Katie. "I'm impressed. Ethan loves all these games."

"Thanks." Katie ducked her head, her asymmetrically cut black hair falling across her face and the gold ring in one nostril gleaming. "I can show him some tricks to beat the game faster."

Katie pushed off the arm of the chair and sat cross-legged in front of the TV with the kids.

Jase came in from the Coburns' kitchen with a sparkling water for his fiancée, Nina, who was expecting a baby—not Jase's. Her ex-fiancé had been one of Tempest's superagents before he'd gone off the rails and died.

Nina smiled her thanks and patted the cushion beside her. "Sit. I'm fine. I don't need anything else."

Jase perched on the edge of the sofa next to her as if he expected her to go into labor at any minute. He hunched forward toward Jack. "Do you believe Correll that Haywood was Caliban? Or do you think he was covering for himself?"

"I'm not sure. The way Correll bungled that—" he glanced at Ethan "—job in Colorado, I find it hard to believe he was the mastermind behind all the chaos Tempest created, or even second in command behind Haywood. Besides, there was definitely someone trying to ensure his cooperation by sending him those pictures and video. Whether or not that person was Haywood is going to require more research on our part."

"Is he giving up any information in prison?" Lola, Jack's wife, came up behind Claire and ran a hand down the back of her hair. "Sorry, sweetie."

Claire twisted her head over her shoulder. "Do you think I care that Spencer's in prison where he belongs? He should be there for what he did to my mother, too, but the authorities told me there's not enough evidence, even the passing reference he made implicating himself in that phone call. But that's okay. I know in my heart that I got justice for Mom, and the rest of the world now knows him for the lying psychopath he really is."

"I know you don't care about Correll. I'm sorry Jack and I doubted you at first."

Claire turned and hugged her longtime friend. "You sent Mike my way, and I'll always be grateful for that."

Jack snorted. "Yeah, Prospero has become a regular dating service, and in answer to your question *mi amor*, Senator Correll has lawyered up and is keeping mum—so far. We do know he was in contact with the man who beat up Fiona. I think that was more personal than anything else."

"And Hamid?" Claire twisted her fingers in front of her. "Can you tie him to Hamid's death?"

Jack lifted a shoulder. "I think Hamid knew more than he'd been telling you, Claire. When he agreed to meet with you, Tempest had to take him out. I'm sure Correll gave that order, too."

Jase jumped up from the sofa. "Then Caliban could still be out there, and we still haven't found the Oxford Don."

Mike glanced at Claire. "Donald Yousef is not going to be able to hide out for long, and if the real Caliban is out there, we've completely de-fanged him."

Jack said, "Mike's right. We've even brought in most of the Tempest superagents."

"Did I ever thank you for the use of your pala-tial estate?" Mike clapped Jase on the back, and Claire knew he was trying to change the subject from Don Yousef.

"Not really. And how did a poor boy from the wrong side of the tracks manage to identify the most expensive bottle of wine in the kitchen?"

Mike jerked his thumb toward Claire. "I had help from the upper-crust broad."

Jase peeked out the curtains. "Someone's com-ing—tall guy and a petite blonde."

"It must be Max Duvall and Ava Whitman." Lola put her glass down on the coffee table next to her husband. "I invited them. Jack's going to talk to Max about working for Prospero."

Liam popped his head up from the game con-troller. "Is that a good idea, Jack? The guy was one of Tempest's superagents."

"So was Simon." Nina rubbed her pregnant belly. "They were duped."

"Shh." Lola put a finger to her lips as the doorbell chimed, and she headed into the foyer to greet them.

The conversation lulled when a tall man with black hair and wary dark eyes entered the room with a woman his polar opposite—all blond sunshine and light.

She took the initiative. "Hi, all. I'm Ava. This is Max. Hope you don't mind that we crashed your Christmas party."

Lola hugged the perky blonde and shook hands with Max as the others in the group waved or got up to shake hands with the newcomers.

Ava held up a bottle of Patrón. "I brought a bottle of tequila for a peace offering just in case any of you still think our loyalties lie with Tempest."

"Tequila?" Katie hopped up from the floor. "Why didn't you say so when you walked in?"

Her lame joke broke the tension, and soon all the adults in the room were talking business.

After several minutes, Lola tapped her wineglass with a fork. "You know, you guys live with this stuff 24/7. It's Christmas, or at least five days after Christmas. Let's enjoy the holiday and each other's company without the darkness intruding."

"You heard the good doctor and lady of the house." Jack clapped his hands. "Eddie, take the kids to the playroom and weed out those violent games for the younger ones. Liam, dude, put some football on and start pouring the shots."

Mike came up behind Claire and curled his arms around her waist. "Is this crazy enough for you?"

"Me? Aren't you going to miss it all?"

"They'll still invite me to their parties." He entwined his fingers with hers. "Come outside with me for a minute. I have a Christmas present for you."

"You've already given me the best gift of all." She kissed him but allowed him to pull her outside into the Florida sunshine.

Mike squinted in the brightness. "I guess we had our white Christmas in Colorado."

"It was the best Christmas of my life. The Chadwicks will never forget what you did for Ethan. They wouldn't have been able to endure another loss."

"You didn't let on how easy the rescue was, did you?"

"Mike." She trailed her fingers across his clean-shaven face. "It wasn't easy for you. You gave up the opportunity to foil the White House plot."

"You heard Liam. It was nothing." He took a flat package, wrapped in glittering Christmas wrap, from behind his back. "Here's your gift."

With a thrill of excitement, she ripped off the paper. She held up a poster board of a large circle with lines crisscrossing the center and moons and stars and astrological signs. "What is this?"

"It's an astrological chart from Madam Rosalee. She did one for you and one for Fiona."

She held it up. "I love it, but what does it all mean?"

"You see this line here?"

"Yes."

"That one means you'll meet a tall, dark stranger and fall in love."

"Really."

"This one means you'll have three children."

"Three? I'd better get busy, then. I've got two to go."

He waggled his eyebrows up and down. "We can get started on that right away."

She rubbed her knuckles across his dark hair, still growing in. "And the two lines that cross here? What do they mean?"

"They mean you'll live happily ever after with the man of your dreams, once you find him."

"You mean that tall, dark stranger?" She threw her arms around his neck. "I've already met him, and I'm ready. I'm ready for my happily-ever-after."

* * * * *